The Sins of Castel Du Mont

Rosemary Bracco Greenbaum Kohler

trimarkpress

Library of Congress Cataloging-in-Publication Data

The Sins of Castel Du Mont

Rosemary Bracco Greenbaum Kohler

P. CM.
ISBN: 978-0-9904211-8-4
Library of Congress Control Number: 2014951673

B15
10 9 8 7 6 5 4 3 2 1
First Edition
Printed and Bound in the United States of America

A Publication of TriMark Press, Inc.
368 South Military Trail
Deerfield Beach, FL 33442
800.889.0693
www.TriMarkPress.com

Dedication

This book is dedicated to my Grandfather Joseph, who had the insight to purchase "The Haunted Castel" of his dreams!

And to my father, John, and mother, Daisy, who in spite of The Castel's history, gifted my sister and me with ten years of luxury, amidst walls with gold and leaf moldings, marble floors, twenty-four carat door-knobs, paintings and numerous frescos.

The appreciation of beauty and art has been with us ever since.

—*Rosemary Bracco Greenbaum Kohler*

Author's Note

Folklore is the soul of places and humans. Without a soul, no one can exist.

I finished this book around 1970, but felt that the people of the town were not yet prepared to accept what had occurred centuries ago without feeling a sense of guilt.

Today, for the new generation—with its exposure to television and computers and its open mind and clearer understanding of life—this saga can now be told.

—*Rosemary Bracco Greenbaum Kohler*

Acknowledgments

In all my excitement, I must not be remiss and forget to thank the following individuals:

Antonio Antoniotti and his wife, Maria (my cousin), for their great help and sworn secrecy until publication).

Hermine Furman, for her patience and help in setting up my story in book form.

Roberta Eberling, my friend and confidant, for her encouragement and contribution to the last edition of the book.

Barry Chesler and the staff of TriMark Press, for their undivided attention, patience and response to my unprofessional questions. Thank you for guiding me through the trials and tribulations of publishing the book.

Without your help, this book might never have been published.

This sketch depicts the way the Castel looked circa 1600 AD. The artist had done intensive research on the original history of the Castel. This presents the back of the fortress-style castel, surrounded by a moat and with a large wooden plank, set down for people to enter. The walk led to a large opening that would bring one to the courtyard, in front of the abode. At night, the plank over the moat was pulled up to ensure safety. The two lookout towers were manned by guards at all times.

Table of Contents

Prologue & History

BOOK ONE

Table of Contents

BOOK TWO

Table of Contents

BOOK THREE

Table of Contents

BOOK FOUR

The Sins of
Castel Du Mont

Prologue

I was born in a castle and have been told, ever since I could remember, that I had been the first legitimate child born there! I did not know what it meant, but it sounded so important that I would repeat it to all who would listen.

Utilizing my poetic license, I shall hereon refer to my place of birth as *The Castel Du Mont* or simply, "The Castel." I changed the name of the castle, as not to embarrass the present church ministry.

In 1402, the Vatican requested of Count of Savoy, the reigning king of the House of Savoy, permission to build a castle in a fortress style. It would be used as a stopover for the church ministries, when traveling on the original road built by The Romans. This was the last stop before driving through the St. Bernard Pass under Mount Blanc, then on through France.

The Castel took several years to build. In the early spring, Moors from Algeria and slaves from other parts of Africa were imported to Piedmont to do the heavy work. Unable to take the cold winter, they were sent back in late autumn, to return in early spring. They built this edifice on top of a hill, in a 'U'-shaped fortress that hugged the church, protecting it.

A high wall and deep moat also surrounded it. Its bridge was set down in the morning to allow the inhabitants, normal traffic and merchants to enter. The bridge was raised at sundown.

The inhabitants lived in stone houses outside The Castel's walls, but were also surrounded by a high wall. The walls of The Castel measured thirty-six to forty inches deep, keeping the rooms cool in summer and warm in winter. It is quite modern—ceramic pipes were set in the walls for cool running water.

A large deep well had been built that the Moors used for centuries to fill the water tower that supplied the water power that fed the ceramic pipes.

Around the 1750s, the original castle burned down. During the 1870s, the inside of The Castel was restored, this time in a modern, renaissance style, a bit more formal than the original fortress style. The rooms were decorated with beautiful frescoes, the bedrooms with silk-damask walls, the ballroom (which held about two hundred people) had twelve doors, all painted light blue with gold trimmings. Only six doors were functional; the rest were just for show.

Rotating fireplaces were installed in most rooms, which were separated into numerous apartments. Private bedrooms and electricity came later, but the wires were set among the frescoes and could hardly be seen. Chandeliers adorned the ceilings, bringing the frescoes to life.

In 1895, the Parisian Count Du Pons, a famous fighter and brave gentlemen of royal blood, married the most beautiful girl in Paris. He loved her so and was so jealous at the thought that any one should take her from him. The Vatican was most thankful for Count Du Pons. In light of numerous contributions he had made to them, it was decided to deed the castle to him.

He took his bride to the castle and insisted she live there, away from the temptations of Paris. In the meantime, he had to return to Paris for months at a time to run his businesses. Things never worked out as planned, for she became pregnant, while he had been gone over six months. Upon learning this, he took her back to Paris and sold The Castel at a great loss.

Around 1900, the mayor of the town purchased The Castel. He had grown-up children, all too old to have a family. My grandfather purchased it in 1918, and I was born there in 1924.

—*Rosemary Bracco Greenbaum Kohler*

*This is The Castel overlooking the village, as it looks today—
the moat, the two lookout towers, and the high wall that
was thrown down after the great deterioration it had suffered.*

*Anyone within a fifty-mile radius will recognize what is
the back of The Castel at first sight. From here on, I will
refer to it as The Castel du Mont.*

History

It was in antiquity, before man appeared on this earth. With the thunderous Adriatic Sea striking its formidable waves against the Alps with winter snows, and spring and summer causing it to recede after so many years, it finally formed this grand and fertile pear-shaped valley, "The Po Valley."

In the extreme north sits the ancient town of Castel Du Mont, set softly between the crowns of the two hills, five-thousand kilometers from the equator. The village is quite antique. Presumably, it has been inhabited for two-thousand years. It is located on the road that went from France via The Mont Cenis Pass in the Alps, through the Province Gallia, into Switzerland. This was the fastest and shortest route for armies and civilians to travel. A golden crucifix had been found there, along with golden coins dating back to Emperor Constantine. The Romans had also made permanent camp here.

In 476, the Roman Empire fell. This particular territory suffered a terrible period with the invasion of the Barbarians. In 568, it was occupied by the original regime of Germany, later known as Lombardy. In the year 700, the French won numerous battles and had acquired so much land that this region was released to Carl Magno, founder of the Sacred Roman Empire.

*Hand-painted frescoes in the bedroom (top photo)
and large ballroom (middle and bottom photos)*

BOOK ONE

CHAPTER ONE

The Castel Du Mont

The original antique castle was built around 800 AD by the Roman Church. They imported black slaves from Africa to work on the building. The work had to be done in the summer because the Moors were not accustomed to the cold winter weather and fell ill during cold seasons. It took several years to complete. The Moors had to return every summer to continue the building process.

A water tower above the roof of The Castel was used to hold the water that ran down ceramic pipes into the interior of this fortress. These pipes still exist today.

After the building was completed, a small number of Moors from Africa remained for the special job of keeping the water tower filled for the inhabitants of The Castel. They were slaves and not allowed to fraternize with the white serfs. A few black women were also imported.

A story has often been told about a beautiful girl named Serafina, who fell madly in love with one of the black slaves. After a secret love affair, she gave birth to a black child. Her mother had smashed the infant's head against the wall before anyone else saw it.

The Castel was a typical Moorish fortress, with two towers perched on a rocky crag on the highest point, surrounded by two moats. The church was built behind it. Both buildings were made of heavy local stones, resulting in strong fortresses for protection against enemies.

The Castel was just another one of the numerous fortresses that the church built after the fall of Constantinople, to defend first the church and its monetary interests, and also the feudal slaves. It was the major stronghold in the countryside, complete with dark cellars and underground galleries.

The signor of the town lived in The Castel with his family. Downhill, across from the first moat, were the homes of the farmers. Water ran between the moats, which were also flanked by a heavy circular wall. There were four large porticos and one little hidden side door known by only a few. It was heavily covered with evergreen vines. The porticos could be opened during the day to let people in and out of the compound. A small fee had to be paid by those who entered. Each portico also had a bridge that was pulled up after dark for the protection of the residents. The last of these bridges were retired in 1733.

The Castel is possessed of knowledge that has been lost in the present generation. Like a woman, it sits at the top of the highest spot, even today. Serenely, yet sternly, it overlooks an aging facade while protecting and guarding the village. The young look upon it as a staunch old lady who remembers its history and mysteries. The old have a much higher regard, respect and love for this most feared and loved establishment.

CHAPTER TWO

Superstitions

In the dark winter, fears and superstitions flourished. Some were real and others stemmed from the imagination. Yet, it was from this illiteracy and nervous idleness that witches could best cast their spells.

The village's witch lived alone in one of the small houses on the edge of the town. She would sit among her talismans and charms made of bones, stones and twigs, which happened to grow in promontory forms to cast her spells. She was always on the lookout for the kind of human being clever enough to become a witch and give her competition. She was essential to the village. People knew they were powerless when the witch turned her face against them.

The Padrone often approached the witch to help him convince his serfs. In this manner, she kept friends with the Padrone and kept the rest of the slaves in their own stupidity. She was much revered and was provided with food and clothing in exchange for her magical favors.

CHAPTER THREE

The Serfs, Renters and Artisans

The Padrone owned all the land, and he allowed his slaves to work it. All products went to him, and they were given some food and lodging for their hard work.

There were also renters living here who were supposed to be free, but the Padrone's high rent required them to work so many hours that, in the end, they were no better off than the slaves.

The artisans who also resided here were free people, just one step better than the renters, although they could grow whatever they wanted on their small parcel of land. They had to pay high taxes to the Padrone for protection, and they were not allowed to sell their products directly on the market. They could sell only to the Padrone, cutting their profits considerably. The houses were built of rocks and stones.

Feudal lords were in frequent discord with other lords and numerous battles were fought.

CHAPTER FOUR

The Pope

In 1307, Pierre Roger was a French Benedictine Abbot, later archbishop, and cardinal called "The Frenchman." He was elected Clement VI, Pope of the Church of Rome. He had visited The Castel Du Mont several times, stopping to rest there during his journeys from Rome to Avignon. He summarily moved the apostolic from Rome to Avignon in his native France, so that he, "his Holiness," might remain near his mistress, who was the wife of Count Perigrid.

He had been away from her for two years in Rome since he had become Pope and, from such a distance, she could not conveniently visit him regularly in the eternal city.

The people looked tolerantly on that temporary aberrance, typical of a Frenchman, except that two years before Clement had been succeeded by another Frenchman. John XXII seemed satisfied that the papal palace remained in Avignon.

Most of Christendom thought this was sacreligious, but to judge from the tempest it raised, especially in the east of Italy in such places as Venice, people were not satisfied. Some suggested that it was unacceptable.

Certainly, St. Peter must have been raging in his Roman catacomb over this.

CHAPTER FIVE

Famine and Black Death at Castel Du Mont

For centuries The Castel Du Mont was war-torn and devastated. It was the worst The Castel had ever suffered. Famine was rampant, and it struck everywhere with more ferocity than the heavy winter's snow and ice that covered the desolate village. Disease was rampant. "The Black Death," a dreaded killing disease, also arrived in this winter of 1347.

A family of twelve or sixteen who was forced to live in one big room, faced the coming winter with only the small food stores that the Padrone had allotted them, and with little hope of finding more. Medicine was unknown and only that which the witch doctor prescribed could be used. But even the witch had never had to fight such a disease before. The house provided no comfort except for a slight protection from the howling of winter winds, which blew almost constantly through the structure.

Children stayed in bed all day because it was the only way to keep warm and survive the winter. Hopefully, they would not be struck down by The Black Plague.

The padrone lived in complete luxury in The Castel, with servants to tend to his every need, warmth from the numerous fireplaces set in each room and abundance of food to fill his large stomach.

People weakened by starvation succumbed to the dreaded disease. It was said that at least three out of four in each family died. With the winter making it impossible to dig in the earth, they had to pile the dead bodies, one above the other, in a large cistern in a far corner of the cemetery. No one was allowed to go near it to mourn because the dangers of being infected were too great.

These winters were long and hard. Soon there would be food only for the young ones and it will be time for the old ones to go, for that was the law of the land. But in this overcrowded house, the aged were greatly revered.

In the Pissinis family this winter, they had already lost four children under five years old, a daughter of seventeen years and the mother. There also was a very old woman to care for who was so precious to them that they would starve themselves, rather than deprive her. She was known as the "Ancient One," and they were determined to help her live out her life because she was the wisest person in the village. She was the only one who could remind the young of their heritage. Others would say "let the old one die," but they had no mind to do so, and they were prepared to stand by the resolute old woman for as long as life remained.

This was difficult for the ancient one. She was not easy to placate and was a burden on her family, but the bond between them was great and indissoluble. When she decided that she had passed on all her knowledge and secrets of healing, she planned one dark evening to sneak out of the house and hide in the woods where the heavy snow and ice storms would make it impossible for anyone, including her family, to find her. It would not be until springtime when someone would find her body atop the hills of the Hebrews, where she planned to spend her last hours, saying goodbye to God.

The French now ruled the village. After fighting numerous battles with the Abbots, they had finally conceded to the Duke of Savoy, and Duke Lomelleux was declared pardone of the town and The Castel.

The young men of The Castel Du Mont, who were constantly called upon to fight in the army to help defend the surrounding territories, were finally returning to their villages to be reunited with their families.

CHAPTER SIX

Bianca

"How long we have awaited your arrival!" As thick red lips briefly touched her fingers, Bianca did not think she liked the Viscount. He had appeared unexpectedly in the chamber where she had just been presented to Count Di Massimo.

The glittering silk-robed Viscount, dazzling with gold embroidery, was too polite to her. He made her feel uneasy, as though there were some hidden purpose to his cordiality. He was tall and heavily built, with long flowing blonde curls, a red face and small red beard.

He bent over her hand with affected charm, while she swept into a deep curtsy. The Viscount straightened and looked into her face with cold blue eyes as he said "But you are exquisite! What a lovely ornament you will be to our court, a treasure I entrust to the care of our Count Di Massimo."

"Thank you my lord." Bianca could not repress a shiver. The Viscount left her and walked out of the room with a mincing gait, accentuating his hulking figure.

Bianca, after a few minutes, transferred all of her attention to Count Di Massimo. He smiled at her, but his eyes were not smiling. They had that sad worried look she had often noticed on lonely men.

He drank much during the king's splendid day-long banquet. Liquor always seemed to loosen the Count's tongue and seemed to facilitate his telling the truth. It was in such a moment that he warned Bianca to keep away from the king, as he had recognized that certain look he gave to the women he commanded to his chambers and forced into a "Menage De Trois" between himself, the lady and the king's male partner. It was quite a combination, but one whose female partner had to be changed nightly.

Bianca panicked, "But what can I do if I am elected?" she asked. "You must take precautions not to be available," answered the Count. "But how?" questioned Bianca.

"First of all, get out of here as soon as possible. Do not go home. He can send you a message there." "But where can I go at this time?" she asked as she panicked.

The Count could see how upset she was. "Go, madam, get your wrap and give this card to your carriage driver. He will drive you to my home. My butler and maids will take care of you for this evening. Hurry now, and go with God." Bianca hurried as if her life depended on it, and in a few seconds she was gone. Unfortunately, that night the king did not have his first choice, and had to call on someone else for his nightly liaisons.

At lunch the next day, she finally met the Count. He had decided to join her for the new meal. "Thank you my lord for saving my life" she exclaimed, "But what can I do now? How can I save myself from this?"

"Easily Madame, you can marry. The king does have some scruples. He will never call on a married woman."

She had become a widow after just two years of an unhappy marriage to a rich merchant from Sienna. His passing left her a very wealthy woman. "Madam, do not worry yourself. You are a most desirable woman. I am certain you can find a husband the moment you decide to do so," he teasingly whispered.

She blushingly rose and excused herself, retiring to her chamber. She knew she had to think. After all, how long could she be a guest of Count Di Massimo? She could not go back to her house and decided to stay on for a limited time as a guest until she was able to make up her mind as to her future.

CHAPTER SEVEN

Count Di Massimo

Count Di Massimo had been born into a famous family but most families of that time were often corrupt. His father had begun to show unmistakable signs of that dementia, which haunted the lives of all of his family.

The infectious syphilis or, perhaps, the general environment in which they lived, began to take its toll on the children in the family. The eldest daughter went into a mental asylum, and her brother followed five years later.

The disease was like a terrifying black shadow, where finally, the darkness closed in taking their minds. The afflicted were removed to what the family now euphemistically called "hospital" to die unseen, almost unnoticed, a few years later.

Bianca had met the Count's father, who resided in a castle in nearby Monza in Lombardy with dozens of servants to help him with his every need.

He was an ancient, paralyzed, blind old creature, whose face had long ago become so fearful with the ravages of his disease. He habitually wore a cloth mask, misshapen, and with a fetid stench, a stink that seemed to catch in the mouth and clog the nostrils.

But Bianca was so blinded by the title that this did not seem to matter. After all, she was not marrying the father.

With Count Di Massimo dressed in the latest fashion and living a rich casual life, there seemed to be no outside signs that anyone could suspect he was developing this condition.

With the passing of her husband, she began wondering whether to marry another old man. They were easier to handle and hopefully died early and left you their money and titles. Count Di Massimo had looked at Bianca with much interest. She was an exciting, sexy woman, and he deserved only the best. He decided to take a wife once more.

For Bianca, taking the battered, yet somewhat virile, Count as her husband was a much thought out plan to fulfill her lifetime ambition and to have a title of nobility. No sacrifice seemed to be too much.

This old aristocratic family had, throughout the last century, lost much of their holdings from bad investments. They were not destitute by any means, but they did not have the great riches of days gone by.

The Count wanted her money and she wanted the title and, most urgently, she wanted to get away from the Viscount's unethical commands.

There was nothing of love in this marriage, in the spasmodic couplings, fights, and the endless recriminations that made up their liaisons. It was hardly bearable from its very beginning.

As fate would have it, Bianca never caught the dreaded disease. After a year of a celibate marriage, she decided to take a few lovers she met in the courts of Milan. These men would have to do for the time being, until she could think of a better alternative, she thought.

Count Alamano Di Massimo hated the life at court. It all seemed so superficial. Being an introverted scholar, he loved his home at The Castel Du Mont, which had been given to him by the Count of Savoy when he had been successful in leading the troops to the Battle of Novarra.

Bianca inflamed him with her ever increasing and open flirtations at court. It insulted his old-fashioned morals and, after much anguish, he decided to move back to The Castel Du Mont.

She was distressed and disillusioned to have to spend some time away from the Milan Courts, for this was her life; it was her love, it was her everything! Yet the Count, upon the marriage, had taken over the management of her money and, without it, she could not function, especially at the court.

Reluctantly, she left for The Castel Du Mont for only one season, with a promise of an early return. She believed him. After all, he was an old man and she was young and beautiful, and he was very much in love with her. She could always cajole him into doing anything she requested. So, the next morning, with all her fancy city gowns and expensive jewelry, and with an entourage of two carriages, they set out for The Castel Du Mont.

The first carriage was completely padded in heavy wine-colored velour and heavy leather springs. The Di Massimo golden crest was etched on its doors, and it was pulled by four handsome white horses. This helped make the trip almost a comfortable one.

The second carriage held all of the Countess' gowns and incidentals.

CHAPTER EIGHT

Bianca and Count Di Massimo

A t The Castel, she befriended Nan, the young bride of Percivalle, her husband's only son.

It was now the end of April and the days were often warm and pleasant. The nightingales had arrived, the cherry and plum trees were in full bloom and the gardens were filled with the sweet scent of purple and white lilacs. Bianca and Nan gaily chatted and laughed and strolled over the green lawns arm and arm, their silk gowns flowing as they admired the raucous-tongued peacocks. In no time at all, they had become fast friends.

Like a woman in love, Bianca was forever talking about Milan. Nan had never been there. Bianca told Nan about the theatres and the towers of the Duomo, the ball and the hawking parties.

For her, Milan was the center of the universe, and whoever was absent from it might as well have been on a distant star.

"Oh, there's nothing so fine" she cried," as to see all the city people at the promenades. Everyone bows and smiles at everyone else. Each time they meet, men lift their hats to the ladies and sometimes, they call out to them, too." She continued to talk as if she were still there.

Nan had always listened with great interest and asked numerable questions, but now she gave an apologetic little smile.

"It sounds very fine, but I think I'd rather hear about it then see it myself."

"What?" cried Bianca, shocked at the blasphemy. "But Milan's the only place in the world to be. Why don't you want to go?"

Nan made a vague deprecatory gesture. She was always acutely conscious of the greater strength of Bianca's personality and it made her feel embarrassed, almost gently, to express an opinion of her own.

"I don't know. I think I would feel strange there. It's so big and there are so many people, and all the ladies are so handsome and wear such fine clothes. I'd be out of place. Why, I'd be lost." Her voice had a timid and almost desperate sound, as though she were already lost in that great terrifying city.

Bianca laughed and slipped one arm about her waist. "Why, Nan, with paint and patches, jewelry and a low-necked gown, you'd be as pretty as anyone! I'll warrant the gallants wouldn't let you alone. They'd be after you day and night."

Nan giggled and her face grew pink, "Oh your ladyship, you know they wouldn't. My heavens! I wouldn't even know what to say to a gallant."

"Of course you would, Nan. You know what to say to Percivalle, don't you? All men are alike. There's just one topic that interests them when they're talking to a woman."

Nan turned red, "Oh, I'm married to Percivalle and he, well…." She changed the subject hastily. "Is it really true what they say about the courts?"

"What do you mean?"

"Oh! You know, they say such terrible things. They say everyone drinks and swears and that even Her Majesty plays cards on Sunday. They say Visconti Della Signoria sometimes doesn't so much as see his wife for months at a time—he is so busy with his other ladies."

"Nonsense, he sees her every day and he is as kind and fond as can be. He says she is the best woman in the world." Nan was relieved, "Then it isn't true that he was unfaithful to her?"

"Oh, yes, he is. All men are unfaithful to their wives. Aren't they, if they get a chance?" But, as Nan looked so stricken, Bianca gave her a little squeeze and added hastily, "Except men who live in the country, they're different."

CHAPTER NINE

Percivalle

At first she had thought Percivalle was different. The instant he had seen her, his eyes lit up with surprise and admiration.

But his father was there, so the looks swiftly passed. After that, she seldom met him, usually only at lunch and supper, when he paid her the same differential consideration she might have expected had she been at least twenty years older. He politely tried to pretend that she was actually nearer his father's age than his own. Bianca finally decided, correctly, that he was afraid of her.

Prompted by boredom, mischief and the desire to revenge herself on Count Di Massimo, she set out to make Percivalle fall in love with her. But she knew the Count well enough to realize that she would have to be cautious and take strictly in private any satisfaction she might find in cuckolding him with his own son.

If he should ever suspect or guess…!!!!! But, she refused to think of that, for nothing vile or cruel seemed beyond the Count. But Percivalle was the only young, personable and virile male at the castle, and she craved the excitement, as well as the flattery, of a man's adoration.

One rainy morning, she met him in the gallery where they stopped to talk about the weather for a moment. He would have gone on almost immediately, but she suggested a game of shuffleboard. While he was trying to find an excuse, she hurried him off to where the table was set. After that, they played cards occasionally. A couple of times, apparently by accident, they met at the stables and rode together. His wife, Nan, was pregnant and could not ride.

But, he continued to treat Bianca like a step-mother and even seemed to be somewhat in awe of her, which was an emotion she was not accustomed to rousing in men, either young or old.

She now saw her husband infrequently—no more often than when living in Milan. He supervised every detail regarding The Castel, which was not attended by the steward, for he refused to allow anyone, especially a woman, to manage his household. He directed the workmen and spent hours in his library. He never rode horseback or played a game or a musical instrument; and, though he was sometimes outdoors, he was never too idle, and always had a definite purpose—when it was accomplished, he returned to The Castel.

He wrote interminably. When Bianca asked him what it was, he told her he was writing the complete history of every article of value he had ever acquired so the family could always know what its possessions were. He also wrote poetry but never offered to read it to her, and she never asked to see it.

She thought writing a very dull occupation and could not imagine a man wasting his time shut up in a dark closed room when outside the white violets were poignantly fragrant, wisterias were hung with purple clusters of bloom, and clean, cool rain swept air and washed over the hills and mountains.

When she tried to quarrel with him about returning to Milan, he told her flatly that she had conducted herself like a fool there and was not fit to live where she would be subjected to temptations.

He repeated that if she wanted to go back alone, he was willing to have her do so, but he reminded her that if she did, she would forfeit all her money to him. She shouted at him in a fury that she would never turn that money over to him, even if she had to stay in the country for the rest of her life. Consequently, convinced that she might be there a long while, she sent for her best friend in Milan to join her. Antonia Ponzini, arrived within a fortnight.

Nan was suffering from morning sickness and never seemed to be well enough to join them. The two friends, as always, seemed to have a great deal to talk about. Both women were interested in the same things, and they gossiped, chattered and exchanged intimate personal details without hesitation or self-conscious laughter.

Innocence and inexperience had begun to bore Bianca, who was relieved to have someone else she could talk to frankly—someone who knew her for exactly what she was and who did not care.

When she told Antonia that she intended seducing her husband's son, Antonia laughed and said there was no limit to a woman's desperation once she was carried off into the country.

Antonia realized for certainty that Percivalle could not bear comparison with the other men Bianca had made love to. As a true, court-thinking woman, she was amused by all of this intrigue.

Antonia's time of departure had arrived. Bianca sadly bade her goodbye and did not waste time getting back to her life at The Castel.

It was not until the middle of May before Percivalle began to seek her out deliberately. She was waiting one morning for her little golden mare to be saddled, when she heard his voice behind her.

"Why, good morning, your ladyship!" You certainly

are riding early!" He tried to sound surprised, but she knew the moment she looked at him that he had come purposely to meet her.

"Good morning, Percivalle. Yes, I think I'll gather some May dew. They say it's the most sovereign thing in the world for a woman's complexion."

Percivalle blushed, grinning at her and whacking his hat nervously against his knee. "Your ladyship can't have need of anything like that."

"What a courtier you are Percivalle!" She looked up at him out of the shadow of her broad hat brim, smiling a little. He doesn't want to, she thought, but he's falling in love with me all the same.

The mare, adorned with a handsome green velvet saddle embroidered in gold lace, was led out of where they stood waiting beneath the great trailing peppered trees. For a moment Bianca talked to the mare, patting her neck and giving her a lump of sugar.

Percivalle then stepped forward to help her mount. She sprang up easily and gracefully.

"We can ride together" she suggested, "Now, unless you were going somewhere to pay a visit."

He pretended to be surprised at the invitation. "Oh! No, no, I wasn't, I was just going to ride by myself. But, thank you, your ladyship. That's very kind. Thank you very much."

They set out over the thick, rolling, clover-covered

meadowland and were presently beyond sight of The Castel. The grass was very wet and the slow-moving herd of cattle grazed in the distance.

For some time neither of them found anything to say but at last, Percivalle called happily, "What a glorious morning it is! Why do people live in cities when there's the country?"

"Why do they live in the country when there are the cities?" asked Bianca.

He looked surprised and grinned broadly showing his even white teeth, "But you don't mean that, my lady, or you wouldn't be at The Castel du Mont."

"Coming to Castel Du Mont wasn't my idea, it was his lordship's." She spoke carelessly. Yet, something of the contempt and hatred she had for the Count must have been in her tone or in some fleeting facial expression, for Percivalle replied quickly as if to a challenge. "My father loves The Castel du Mont. He always has. We never liked living in Milan. His Highness Victorio Amedeo, King of Sardinia, once visited here and said that he thought this was one of the loveliest country castles he had ever seen."

"Oh, it's a mighty fine place, I doubt not," agreed Bianca, aware that she had offended his family loyalty, though she did not very much care. They rode some distance further without speaking.

At last she called to him. "Let's stop here a while!"

Without waiting for his answer, she began to rein in her horse but he rode several hundred yards beyond, wheeled and came back slowly.

"Perhaps we'd better not, since there is no one about."

"What of that?" demanded Bianca in her impatient amusement?

"Well, you see Madame, his lordship thinks it's best not to dismount when we ride. If we were seen, someone might misunderstand. Country people love to gossip."

"People everywhere love to gossip. Well, you do as you like. I am going to get off." And immediately, she jumped down, pulled off her hat, to which she had pinned two or three fresh roses, and shook her hair.

He watched her and then, setting his jaw stubbornly, he dismounted, too. At his suggestion, they stared over to see a pretty little stream that ran nearby.

The brook was noisy. Full, dark green bulrushes grew along the banks, and there were weeping willows that dipped their branches into the water. Through the trees, sunlight filtered down onto Bianca's head, like the light in a cathedral.

She could feel him watching her, surreptitiously, out of the corners of his eyes. She looked around suddenly and caught him. Slowly she smiled and her eyes slanted, staring at him with bold impudence. "What was your father's last duchess like?" she asked him finally. She knew that his own mother, the first Lady Melissa, had died at his birth. "Was she pretty?"

"Yes, a little, I think. At least her portrait is pretty. But she died when I was nine, so I don't remember her very well." He seemed uneasy at being alone with her. His face had sobered and his eyes could no longer conceal what he really felt.

"Did she have any children?"

"Two. They died very young of smallpox; I had it too." He swallowed hard and took a deep breath. "But, I lived."

"I'm glad you did, Percivalle," she said very swiftly. She continued to smile at him, half in mockery, but her eyes were weighted with seduction. Nothing had aroused her so much in over four weeks. Percivalle, however was obviously wretched. His emotions pulled him two ways, desire in one, filial loyalty in another.

He began to talk again quickly, on a more impersonal subject. "What is the court in Milan like now? They say it's most magnificent, and that even foreigners are surprised at the state in which his majesty lives."

"Yes, it is. It's beautiful. I don't think there can be any more handsome men or beautiful women, any place on Earth., When were you last there?"

"Two years ago I spent several months in Milan. When I returned from my travels, many of the paintings and hangings were just the finest." His tongue talked but his eyes were hot and intense, and as he swallowed, she saw the bobbing movement of his Adam's apple in his thick corded neck.

"I think we better start back now," he said. "Suddenly, it's growing late."

Bianca shrugged her shoulders, picked up her skirts and began to make her way back through the tall grass.

CHAPTER TEN

The Game

She did not see him at all the next day. To tease him, she pleaded an attack of the vapors and ate lunch and supper in her own chambers.

He sent up a bouquet of roses with a formal note, wishing for her rapid recovery. When she went out the following morning, she expected to find him at the stables, waiting there like a schoolboy, hanging about the corner, where he hoped his sweetheart might pass.

But he was nowhere in sight and she had a brief angry sense of pique, for she had thought him badly smitten and she had been looking forward, with some excited anticipation, to their next meeting. Nevertheless, she set off alone in the same direction they had taken two days before.

In only a few minutes she had completely forgotten Percivalle and also his father, who was more difficult to force out of her mind, and was wholly engrossed in thoughts of past lovers. Bianca was so absorbed when her horse shied suddenly, she grabbed at the reins and all but sailed over its head. Recovering herself and looking about for whatever had caused the animal's nervousness, she saw Percivalle, red faced and guilty eyed, astride his own horse, by the three sentinel poplars that stood alone in the midst of the meadow.

Immediately he began to apologize for having startled her. "Oh, ladyship, forgive me. I didn't mean to frighten you. I just stopped here for a moment to enjoy the morning when I saw you coming, so I waited." The explanation was made so earnestly that she knew it was a lie and that he had not wanted his father to see them ride off together. Bianca regained her balance and laughed good-naturedly, "Oh, it's you. I was just thinking about you." His eyes shone at that but she stopped any foolish comment he was about to make by saying, "Come on, I'll race you to the stream."

He reached it just ahead of her. When she swung down from the saddle, he immediately followed, making no arguments this time. "How beautiful it is here in May!" she exclaimed, "Why not?" he agreed, bewildered.

"I think I'll sit down. Will you spread your cloak for me Percivalle, so I won't spoil my gown?" She glanced around to find the most pleasant spot.

"Over there against the tree, please." With a display of great gallantry, he swirled off his long riding cloak and laid it on the damp grass. She dropped down easily with her back against the dainty birch and her legs stretched out straight, crossed at the ankles. She flung her hat aside. "Well, Percivalle, how long are you going to stand there. Sit down." She indicated a place beside her.

He hesitated, "Why-ugh—." Then, with a sudden resolve, he said briskly, "Thank you, your ladyship" and sat facing her, with his arms resting on his drawn-up knees.

But instead of looking at her, he kept intent watch on a bee, which was going hurriedly from flower to flower, caressing each surface and lingering occasionally to sip the last bit of honey. Bianca began idly picking the little daisies that grew profusely in the grass and tossing them, one after the other in her lap, until she had a mound of them.

And now he looked directly at her. "It doesn't seem as though you're my step-mother. I can't make myself believe it, no matter how I try. I wonder why?" He seemed genuinely puzzled, so Bianca thought. "Perhaps," she suggested lazily, "you don't want to."

She began to make the flowers into a wreath for her hair, piercing the tiny stems with one sharp fingernail and dexterously threading them together.

He thought that over in silence, and then suddenly blurted out, "How did you ever happen to marry father?" Bianca kept her eyes down, apparently intent on her work.

She gave a little shrug. "He wanted my money and I wanted his title."

When she looked up she saw a worried frown on his face, "What's the trouble," she asked.

"Aren't all marriages a bargain? I have this, you have that." He seemed to be trying to convince himself, more than her, and looked at her tensely.

"He's mighty fine, Count Di Massimo," she said sarcastically.

"He's mighty fond of you too." She gave a burst of impolite laughter at that. "What the devil makes you think so?"

"He told me."

"Did he also tell you to keep away from me?"

"No, but I should. I know I should never have come today." His last words came out swiftly, and he turned his head away.

Suddenly he started to get to his feet. She reached out and caught at his wrist, drawing him swiftly towards her.

"Why should you keep away from me Percivalle?" she muttered. He stared down at her, half kneeling, his breath coming hard. "Because I, . . . because I should. I'd better go now, before I—"

"Before you what?"

The sun through the leaves made a spatter of light and dark upon her face and throat. Her lips were moist and parted and her teeth shone white between them. Her speckled amber eyes held his silently.

"Percivalle, what are you afraid of? You want to kiss me. Why don't you?" And kiss her he did. "Well, unhook me," she whispered.,"

"I don't know how to do it."

"Oh, good heavens." She reached behind her neck, and undid several hooks. "Now, you finish."

Beads of perspiration stood on his forehead and his hands trembled. Without hesitation, she pulled the dress down over her shoulders and slipped her petticoats down with it. After a swift rustle of fabric, she stood clad in the raw. She turned around to face Percivalle in her shining nudity.

He took an uncertain step back, open mouthed, his eyes mesmerized by her tender pink flesh, that he had so often tried to summon to his imagination. Now he understood, woefully, how unequal to the task his imagination had been.

Bianca smiled and stepped closer to him. She let her arms flow outward from her body and stood still for inspection.

Percivalle swallowed hard; he hadn't suspected he'd be so shaken. It was an alarming and intoxicating feast. She moved closer to him and put a hand on his shoulder, "I've wanted to be alone with you for such a long time," she whispered. Her hand crept up on the back of his neck. Her moist lips parted and came toward his and covered them, pressing hard, as her arms wound tightly around his neck. His hands came down and covered her back and pulled her close against him. She breathed a long, soft, yearning sigh and rotated her mouth hard on his. She sighed again with greater joy, as she felt him responding.

His breathing became heavier and his hands roamed eagerly over her back, from shoulders, to waist, to buttocks and back again. After a while she turned her head and stood with lifted face and closed eyes, while he dropped tiny kisses like rose petals on her eggshell ears and slender neck.

"Your ladyship, your ladyship," his voice was husky, low and trembling, "Oh God, it's crazy, your ladyship. It cannot be."

"It can be. It can be and it will be," she murmured in a determined whisper. She watched him as his eyes roamed over her body, inch by inch—over her hips, her bushy black pubic region, her gracefully curved waist that led up to her fine, prominent breasts, and when he reached her face, she smiled down at him. He held his arms slightly away from her body. She unbuttoned his shirt and pulled it off and as she opened his trousers, loosened his underwear and pushed his clothing down to the ground, kneeling as she did so. He stepped out of them, naked. Then from the kneeling position, she raised her face to the level of his extended erection, caressed it with her fingers, her lips and her mouth, as he stood rigidly still, looking at her with his hand on her head.

His breathing became labored as she worked. He perspired, he quivered, and at last he clutched at her. "All right, Bianca, enough." He bent down and pulled her away from himself and helped her to the ground.

She lay there, arms and legs sprawled, and he came over her and nestled on the soft broad cushion of her body. Under his gaze, her amber eyes sparkled and her white teeth gleamed. "How beautiful you are," he murmured. His hands immediately went to her breasts again and fondled them, while he kissed her repeatedly with movement of his lips.

Bianca's head swayed gently from side to side as if to music. Her eyes were drugged, and her legs opened wider and came around him. Her hand groped and guided him into herself.

At first he moved slowly and gently, but soon the rhythm quickened. She moaned as the rhythm increased to a full crescendo and, with a swift thrust, he released her, and fell exhausted over her.

Afterwards, they lay quietly. He sighed with deep weariness. He had not experienced such pleasure in a long time. He turned to her and in a most disappointing voice, softly muttered, "We must get dressed and return to the cold, hard castle." Percivalle's conscience troubled him at first as he tried to avoid his step-mother.

The day after she had seduced him, he went to visit a neighbor and remained away for almost a week. When he returned he was so busy visiting tenants that he seldom appeared, even for meals. On those occasions when he could not avoid meeting her, his manner was exaggerated, stiff and formal. Bianca was angry, for she thought that his ridiculous behavior would give them both away. Furthermore, he was the one source of amusement she had found in the country and she had no intentions of losing him.

One day from the windows of her bed chamber, she saw him walking alone across the terrace from the garden. Her husband was in the library and had been there for some time, so she picked up her skirt and rushed out of the room, down the stairs and onto the stone terrace. Percivalle was below. But as she started after him, he glanced hastily around and dodged into a tall maze of clipped hedges that had been planted about fifty years before. It had grown so tall, that it was almost possible to get lost there. She reached it, looked about, but could not see him. Then she ran in, turning swiftly into one lane after another and came up against a blank wall. She retraced her steps to start down another path.

"Percivalle," she cried angrily. "Percivalle, where are you?" But he made no answer. Then, all at once, she turned into a lane and found him. He was caught, for it was closed at the end. He glanced uneasily about him, saw that there was no escape, and faced her with a look of guilty nervousness. Bianca burst into laughter.

"Oh, you silly boy. What do you mean running away from me like that? You'd think I was a monster!"

"I wasn't," he protested, "I wasn't running away, I didn't know you were there."

She made a face at him. "You've been running away from me for two weeks now, ever since . . . "

He looked at her with such protesting horror that she stopped, widening her eyes and raising her brows. "Well," she breathed softly, "then what's the matter? Didn't you enjoy yourself? You seemed to at the time."

Percivalle was in agony, "Oh, please, your ladyship, don't. I can't stand it. I'm going out of my head. If you talk that way, I'll . . . I don't know what I'll do."

Bianca put her hands on her hips and one foot began to tap impatiently. "Good lord Percivalle, what's the matter with you? You act as if you've committed some crime!" Her eyes rose again.

"I have!"

"What, for heavens sake?"

"You know what," protested Percivalle.

"I don't!"

"Ah! We've committed adultery!" he protested.

"Adultery is no crime, it's an amusement." She was thinking he was a fine example of the folly of allowing a young man to live so long in the country, shut away from polite manners.

"Adultery is a crime! It is a crime against two innocent people, your husband and my wife. But, I've committed a worse crime than that. I've made love to my father's wife. I've committed incest." The last word was a whisper, and his eyes stared at her full of self-loathing.

"Nonsense, Percivalle, we're not related. That was a law made up by old men for protection of older men, silly enough to marry young women. You're making yourself miserable for nothing."

"Oh, I'm not, I swear, I'm not. I've made love to other women before, plenty of them. But I've never done anything like this. This is bad and wrong. You don't understand. I love my father a great deal; he's a very fine man. I admire him and now, what have I done?" He looked so thoroughly wretched that Bianca had a fleeting sense of pity for him; but, when she reached over to press his hand, he stepped back as if she were something poisonous. She shrugged her shoulders.

"Well, Percivalle, it'll never happen again. Forget about it. Just forget it ever happened."

"I will. I've got to."

But she knew that he was not forgetting at all and that, as the days went by, he would find it more and more difficult to forget. She did nothing to help him, which seemed just as effective as anything more flagrant could possibly have been by the end of the fortnight.

He met her again when she had gone out to ride, and, after that, he was completely helpless in his feelings of guilt and self-hatred. But the desire for pleasure was stronger.

They found many places to meet. Like all great old castles, The Castel Du Mont was full of hiding places that had once been used for concealing the actions of priests and nuns. There were window seats which might be lifted to disclose a small room below and corner fireplaces that swiveled into three other rooms. Percivalle knew them all. For Bianca, at least, all these various hidden rendezvous afforded a dangerous excitement from which she derived far more enjoyment than she did from Percivalle's inept lovemaking.

She did not, however, find it so amusing, that she was less eager to return to Milan. She asked Count Di Massimo, over and over again, when they were going back to Milan. Invariably, he said he had no plans for returning at all. He would as soon stay in the country until he died.

"I'm bored out here!" she shouted at him. "I doubt you are, Madame," he said. "In fact, it's always been puzzling to me how women avoid boredom wherever they are. They have so few resources."

"We have resources enough," Bianca said, giving him a slanted look of venom and contempt. She started the conversation with good resolutions, but they could not last under his cold supercilious stare and his sneering sarcasm. "But it's dull out here. I couldn't wish the devil himself a worse fate than to be boxed up in this castle."

"You should have considered that, when you were attempting to prostitute yourself in court." His whole decadent figure leaning against a large window was like that of delicate porcelain. She longed to smash her fist against the fragile bones of his cheeks and nose and skull and feel them crumble beneath her knuckles. "I cannot undo Madame the faults you've committed before I married you, but I can at least prevent you from committing new ones now."

For an instant, fury brought her close to a disastrous error. It was on the end of her tongue to tell him about herself and Percivalle, to prove to him that he could not govern her life, no matter how he tried. But just in time, she controlled herself and said, instead, with an unpleasant sneer, "Oh! Can you?"

Di Massimo's eyes narrowed as he spoke to her. He measured each word like a precious poison. "Someday, madam, you'll try me too far. My patience is long, but not endless."

"And then my lord what will you do?"

"Go to your room!" he said suddenly. "Go to your room, madam, or I shall have you carried there by force."

Bianca felt that she would burst with rage and raised her clenched fist to strike him. But he stood so imperturbably and looked to her so coldly, that though she hesitated for several seconds, she at last muttered a curse, turned and ran out of the library.

Her hatred for her husband was so intense that it ate into her brain. He observed her day and night until it became a torment which seemed unendurable. She began to scheme how she might get rid of him; she wanted him dead.

She had never tried to understand him or what made him the kind of person he was, for they not only disliked each other, but found each other mutually un-interesting.

One night in August, she was considering which gown she would wear the following day; they were expecting a number of guests, most of them Nan's relatives, who were coming to spend a few days with them. Bianca was delighted at the opportunity it would give her to show off, and did not doubt that they would be vastly impressed, for they were all people who lived in the country. Most of the women had not ever been to Milan or at court.

CHAPTER ELEVEN

The Wedding Gown

Bianca and Nan were going through the tall standing cabinets in which her clothes were kept. "Look Nan, here is the white satin embroidered gown my husband had requested I wear on my wedding night." Both of them looked it over critically, as Bianca mused "I wonder who it belonged to?"

"Maybe his lordship's first duchess. Why don't you ask him sometime?"

"I think I will."

At 10 o'clock, her husband came upstairs from the library. That was the hour when they usually went to bed and he was consistent in his habits, faithful to each smallest one. This was a characteristic of which she and Percivalle had taken full advantage.

He had never once allowed her to see him naked, nor did she wish to. When he returned from the bathroom, he was wearing a handsome dressing gown made of fine East Indian silk. He picked up a snuffer and started around the room to put the candles out.

"The old white satin gown," she said idly, "is the one you wanted me to wear when we were married. Where did you get it? Who wore it before I did?"

He paused and in the mid-darkness, she could see him looking at her, smiling reflexively. "It's strange you haven't asked me that before. However, there seems to be few enough decencies between us. I may as well tell you it was intended to be the wedding gown of a young woman I once expected to marry, but did not."

Bianca raised her eyebrows, unmistakably pleased. "Oh! So you were jilted."

"No, I was not jilted. She disappeared one night during the siege of her family's castle. Her parents never heard from her again, and we were forced to conclude that she had been captured and killed."

He seemed profoundly sad and yet obviously deriving some measure of gratification from recalling the past. "She was a very beautiful, kind and generous woman—a lady. Incredibly as it may seem, the first time I saw you, I was strongly reminded of her. You don't look like her—only a very little—and, certainly, you have none of the qualities which I admired in her." He gave a faint shrug. He went on snuffing the candles. The last one went out and the room was suddenly dark.

"I had been looking for her for years in the face of

every woman I've seen, everywhere I've gone. I've hoped that perhaps she wasn't dead, that someday, somewhere, I'd find her again. But now, I've ceased looking. I know that she is dead."

"So you were in love once!" She said, angry to know he had once been able to love another woman with tenderness and generosity.

"Yes, I was in love once, only once. I remember her with the manner in which a young man idealizes, and I still love her!"

"Did you not love your first wife, Percivalle's mother?" She asked. "No, my dear; that, too, was our own marriage—a marriage of convenience. She was young and I had to have an heir!" In a few minutes she could hear his heavy breathing of sleep.

Nan's relatives stayed for several weeks. They were interested in Bianca's gowns and jewels, though none of them approved of her.

She was happy when these relatives finally left, for by now, they found her exciting as they dwelled on her tales of glamorous court life. But Bianca missed the company of masculine suitors. She missed having someone paying court to her and she missed, most of all, the excitement of lovemaking.

She now set out to work Percivalle to such a pitch of infatuation and resentment that it would be difficult for him to use discretion.

CHAPTER TWELVE

Poisonous Revenge

"What are we going to do with him? I hate him now. Last night I met him in the gallery. He was going into you. My God, for a minute I thought I was going to grab him by the throat," Percivalle sighed heavily.

A few days later, Bianca came into the house alone from her morning ride—Percivalle had returned from another route so that they would not be seen together—and she found the Count at the writing table in their bedroom. "Madam" he said, speaking to her over his shoulder, "I find it necessary to pay a brief visit to Milan. I'm leaving this afternoon, immediately following lunch."

A quick smile sprang over Bianca's face, "Oh! Wonderful, your lordship! I'll send Meg packing right now!"

"Don't trouble yourself. I'm going alone."

"Alone? But why should you? If you're going, I can go, too!"

"I shall be gone but a few days. It's a matter of

important business, and I don't care to be troubled with your company."

Bianca yelled after him, "I won't stay, I won't! I won't!" as the door closed behind him. "The bastard," she hissed.

When she changed her clothes and was ready to go, she discovered that the doors leading into the gallery had been locked from the other side and that her own key was not to be found. At last, in a passionate temper, she began smashing everything she could lay her hands on.

After a while someone opened the door into the entrance hall and slid a tray full of food in, wrapped on the door to call her attention, and then ran off down the gallery. Bianca grabbed up the cold fowl and flung it across the room, then shoved away the tray and dishes, causing a large crash across the marble floor.

After about fifteen minutes, she became aware of a muffled pounding and a woman's faint cries. It was Nan hammering at the outer door.

"Your ladyship, your ladyship!" screamed Nan, and there were hysterical tears in her voice.

"Here I am, Nan! What's happened? What's the matter?"

"It's Percivalle! He's desperately sick! I'm afraid he's dying. Oh, your ladyship, you've got to come!"

A chill of horror ran over Bianca. Percivalle sick? Dying? Only that morning, before the ride, they'd been in the summerhouse and he had been perfectly well.

"What's the matter with him? I can't get out Nan! I'm locked in! Where's the Count?"

"He's gone! He left three hours ago! Oh, Bianca you've got to get out! He's calling for you!" Nan began to sob.

"Get the footman! Make them break open the door. Is he there?"

"He's here, but he says he doesn't dare unlock the door. The Count left orders not to let you out no matter what happens!"

"Open this door you valet, open it or I'll set fire to the house!" She smashed furiously against the lock with a brass shovel. There was a long moment of hesitation after which the man began to pound at the door from the outside while Bianca stood waiting, wet with sweat. At last, the lock broke and she burst out. She flung an arm around Nan's waist and started down toward the end of the gallery where Percivalle's apartments were located. Percivalle was lying on the bed, still fully dressed. But, a blanket was over him and his face contorted almost beyond recognition. He was writhing and turning, clutching at his stomach, his teeth ground together until the veins on his neck seemed ready to burst.

He looked at her for a moment without recognition. Then he grabbed her by the wrist, pulling her toward him. "I've been poisoned!" His voice was a harsh whisper. Bianca gasped in horror, staring backward, "Have you eaten anything today?"

Suddenly she realized what had happened. The Count had found out about them and had tried to poison both of them. The food sent up on her tray must have been poisoned. She felt sick and dizzy and cold, and wept with selfish anxiety.

There was an explosive spitting sound from beneath the blankets and Percivalle's body leaped upward in convulsion. He threw himself from side to side, as though trying to escape the pain. Agonized paroxysms jerked at his face. It was several moments before he could speak.

"Pains began half hour ago. The summerhouse! There's a hollowed eye in that stone mask on the wall...." He could say nothing more. Nan was close beside them. Count Di Massimo could have been there that morning, watching them.

Loathing and helpless rage filled her. But there was relief, too. Because she was not poisoned, she was not going to die. She could see Percivalle's face in its agony and hear the hoarse, desperate sound of his voice.

Percivalle was buried that same night as dusk settled through a brilliant sunset sky. The family chaplain who had baptized him administered the last sacraments and conducted the services. Bianca and Nan and some of the servants knelt in silence. For the pride of family loyalty, they told all others that he had accidentally shot himself while cleaning a gun.

Neither Bianca nor Nan wanted to be alone that night, and Nan was having spasmodic cramps, which she feared might mean that her labor had begun prematurely. They stayed together in a seldom-used apartment, for they were both reluctant to return to their own apartments. Bianca was determined she would never go back to hers again as long as she lived.

By ten o'clock Nan's pains had stopped and she went to bed. Bianca stayed up, nervous and jumpy, apprehensive of shadows, and alarmed at any unexpected sounds. She felt as though hideous, unseen things surrounded her on every side, shutting her in until she could scarcely breathe. Once, she screamed out loud with terror. She kept all of the candles she could find lit and refused to take off her clothes.

In the morning Nan awoke. "Oh, Bianca, you did not sleep."

"No, Nan, I could not. I made up my mind. Today I am leaving here. Your mother is due here tomorrow. I must go!"

With Bianca gone, Nan would nervously await her mother's arrival. No child had ever been born in The

Castel due to lack of proper facilities, and she had to get to the hospital in Torino for the birth. Her mother's arrival would put Nan at ease, knowing she was once more in good hands.

CHAPTER THIRTEEN

Milan Once More

She could not and would not tell Nan where she was going, but she knew very well herself. For now, the chance had come for all the plans she had mulled and brooded over these past weeks to fall into place. She had expected to use Percivalle, but now that he was dead, she realized that she could do it better without him. She intended that the Count had to die since now it was either his life or hers.

Nan wept and begged her over and over to change her mind, but when Bianca refused, she helped her get ready and gave her many admonitions about taking care of herself.

"There's one thing I'll never be able to understand. Count Di Massimo is not a nice person and never seemed to like me," Nan said, as she watched Bianca dressing for her trip. "I don't know why he saved me. If he wanted to kill you and Percivalle, why would he have let me live?"

Bianca gave her a swift narrowed glance, and as the blood rushed into her face, she bent her head. Poor innocent little Nan. She still did not know, and certainly it could do her no good to know. "He would not kill you Nan, because you are carrying his grandchild! He needs someone to carry on his name and title." With this answer, Nan seemed to be satisfied.

Bianca stood bathed in light coming through the window. With her chin raised as she gazed out upon the rolling fields and snowcapped mountains. She held the smile of one confident of her goals in life. She leaned forward and looked intently out of the window. Her movement brought Nan to her side. "I wish you wouldn't leave," she pleaded.

"Here is my carriage. I'm sorry, Nan, but I must go. Goodbye dear one."

The carriage was just topping the lowered bridge of the moat and rolling into the courtyard. Bianca was anxious to be on her way. The dapple-gray horses tossed their noble heads and pranced to a halt. Pierre, like any good coachman, jumped down and swung open the door of the coach.

Bianca glanced up at the sky and experienced a new anxiety. The dark clouds had gathered in the deepening dusk almost into night. It had been raining for hours. Her dread of storms had plagued her since she was a child, and even now, as a woman, she could not subdue her fear. Hearing a light rumbling of thunder, she cringed inwardly. The wind began blowing about. It rose forlornly and whistled eerily at a higher pitch as raindrops splattered all about in heavy downpour streams.

She hurried as the coachman helped her to the carriage. She cuddled up, all alone, and seemed to be a very small, quiet and forlorn figure. The carriage swung down the gulley-washed road, as lightning flashed and thunder echoed across the hills. Bianca flinched with each shattering explosion of sound, as the jagged light streaked across the darkened sky.

The ride was intolerably long. The rain beat monotonously upon the roof, deadening all other sounds, while lanterns lent only a weak flickering light to the ebony darkness through which it passed.

Though the luxurious interior was warm, snug, and well protected from the miserable night, Bianca was hardly comfortable. Her dash to the coach had been shear folly. Her shoes were soaked, her knee length stockings were damp, almost to their full length, and the wet hem of her skirt was cloyingly cold and chilly against her ankles. Gathering the sodden cloak about her, she huddled in its folds and could not suppress a shiver or stop her teeth from chattering. She sat in the corner, her back against the side of the carriage. The small lantern inside the coach gave off a soft dim light.

That night she spent at a roadside inn. In the morning, the road behind seemed to be alive with dark green fields along the great ridge of the Alps, which lay like a serrated crown along Italy's head. They were driving along the Po Valley, hemmed on one side by the Grand River Po and on the other side by the majestic Alps, still covered with snow, soaring to the sky.

Finally, it stopped raining and the sun shone brightly. Ox wagons gave place to a hampered pack of mules, herds of jerkily trotting goats and narrow high-wheeled donkey carts. Peasants crossed themselves at the tiny roadside mini-chapels, spotted intermittently along the roads. The quick dabs of their fingers across the chest and foreheads were more in the nature of signs, warding off ill luck, than symbol affirmations of the Christian faith. The view was truly breathtaking.

Along the High Plateau of the Vercelli Valley, the cool air smelled of pine trees, mountains and grass, as a breeze blew brightly through the stuffy carriage.

Then down once more to the valley of Novarra, the carriage almost came to a stop, hindered by a quantity of interested cows. Below the valley one could see the numerous rice fields, so popular in this part, as one enters the state of Lombardy.

At the end of the valley, the carriage began to climb as the road curveed up in great loops, leaving the fields and orchards, the vineyards and little towns scattered like toys on the valley floor, to bask in the last of their long hot breathless Italian afternoon under the western sky. Another range of mountains were purple under the falling sun, with the Army cemetery's banner floating above the regimented rows of white crosses. After one more full day of riding, they suddenly entered the state of Lombardy, stretching flat and golden into the late afternoon haze.

The sky darkened once more, and lightning set the sky ablaze. But this was not the home country. Milan was somewhere ahead. It was almost the end of the road. The coach lurched into a faster motion as they galloped. The rain finally stopped and she fell asleep. The rest of the trip to Milan was uneventful. At last, after three days, she reached the Di Massimo Villa in the center of Milan. She rapped at the front door and a footman answered. "Where is your master?" she asked. He gave her a surprised look and with a jerk of his head, said, "Upstairs, I think, in his bedroom. Should I announce you, my lady?"

She shoved him aside and rushed up the steps and hurried down the long gallery, whose walls were completely covered with famous masterpieces of art. She continued to his lordship's apartments. She turned around and looked at the footman as she said, "Don't come back here until we call you!" and then walked swiftly across the parlor toward the bedchamber.

"My lord," Bianca's voice rang out like a tolling bell. There was a single candle burning on the table beside him, but a glare of the flames lighted the room brilliantly.

"It's you?" he asked, with great surprise.

"Yes, it's me and alive. No ghost, my lord. Percivalle is dead, but I'm not."

The incredulity on his face shifted at last to a kind of horror. In his moments of madness, had he killed his only child and not her? One look at his grieving face and, suddenly, Bianca's fears were gone. She felt powerful and strong and filled with loathing that brought out everything cruel and fierce and wild in her.

She started toward him, walking slowly. She picked up a riding whip that was on a table nearby in her right hand and flashed it nervously against her leg. He stared at her, her eyes straight and steady. He looked distraught, and muscles around his heart twitched ever so slightly. "My son is dead!" he repeated slowly, fully realizing for the first time what he had done. "He's dead and you're not." He looked beaten and older than ever before, all his confidence gone. The murder of his son had completed the ruin of his life.

"So, you finally found out about us!" taunted Bianca. He smiled a faint and reflective smile, cold, contemptuous, and strangely sensual. Slowly he began to answer "Yes. Many weeks ago I watched you together, there in the summer house—thirteen times in all. I watched what you did and listened to what you said, and I got a great deal of pleasure from thinking how you would die one day, when you least expected it!?"

"Did you?" she snapped her voice taunt and hard, as the candle's wick flickered back and forth, swift as a snake, "but I didn't die, and I'm not going to die."

Her eyes flared to a wild blaze. Suddenly, she raised the whip and lashed it across his face with all the force in her body. He jerked backward, but the first blow left a thin red welt from his left temple to the bridge of his nose. She struck at him again and again, so blind now with rage that she could scarcely see.

Suddenly he grabbed hold of the candlestick and plunged it toward her, having all his weight behind it. She moved swiftly aside and, as she dodged, and gave a shrill scream. The candlestick struck her shoulder and bounced off. She saw his gauche face loom close as his hand seized the whip. They began to struggle and, just as Bianca brought up her knee and kicked him hard in the groin, she picked up the candlestick he had dropped and, with it, hit him hard several times over his head. The Count lay sprawled grotesquely on the floor, his naked head streaming with blood. A strong revulsion swept her. She felt no pity or regret but only a violent paroxysm of satisfied rage and hatred.

All at once, she became aware that the draperies were on fire and, for a horrified moment, she realized that the house was burning and she was trapped. Then she saw that the candle he had thrown at her had fallen beside the window. The draperies had caught fire and now flames roared to the ceiling and licked along to the wooden molding. She went clattering nosily down the little back staircase. Halfway down she met the butler, who pushed past her.

"Fire!" she shouted at him. "The house is on fire!" Instantly, he rushed up to save the Count, but realized it was in vain. The flames were all about. He turned and ran down the steps.

She ran down and stumbled into the courtyard. She glanced around once and saw that the flames from the upstairs windows already were casting a reflection in the courtyard pool.

She had become a widow once more; now, not only a rich one, but with a title of Countess as well. It did not take Bianca long to reinstate herself in the court of Milan, and now the nightly liaisons with the Viscount was something she looked forward to with much pleasure.

Within two years, she came down with the disease she most dreaded, and spent her last few years on earth, not at court, but in the identical condition as her father-in-law.

The new inhabitants of The Castel Du Mont continued in a more normal, uneventful, and timely lifestyle for the next seventy five years under a complete
serf system.

BOOK TWO

CHAPTER FOURTEEN

Clara

"Clara!" Giovanni, the miller, turned with an excited expression and called again, "Clara, come here. Splendid news." His hands trembled and his thin face was creased into furrows of delight, slightly shaded by a soft white powder from his millwork. His daughter appeared in the doorway. She paused, surveying her father's black boots, completely covered by the white dusty flour.

"Father, you're quite untidy, you know," she observed as her dark skirt brushed lightly against his dusty boots, picking up some of the white flour. Then she stepped cautiously close to him. A fond smile curved Clara's mouth as she approached her father without mishap, and her heavy lashed violet eyes deepened with affection. "What's the good news father?"

"The Padrone wants me to mill the special fine bleached white flour for him for a very special party he is giving."

Dusty spectacles balanced on the tip of Giovanni's nose and his blue eyes were sparkling with glee as he tapped a finger on the table. Reaching out, Clara smoothed back the thinning brown hair that straggled onto his forehead.

"Papa, you really must take better care of yourself," she scolded. But there was no censure in her tone. "You've been working so hard at the mill for weeks and not getting enough to eat or enough rest. Your eyes must rest before you take on any extra work. Are you certain this extra request is good news?"

Waving an impatient hand, Giovanni cut off her rambling scold. "Of course it's good news. The Padrone will pay me handsomely for this."

Since her mother's death, Clara had taken over the job of looking after her father. He told her, "None of that matters. The Padrone expects me to do it, and I will do it. Being the only miller in town, the responsibility falls on my shoulders with no sons to help me and all others have their own work to do. I must do it all, and that is final."

Clara's delicate brows arched in faint surprise, "I can help you, Father."

"True, but you are a woman and women do not work in mills."

"Well, this woman will," she said with grim firmness, and he just smiled.

"Let me think about it. We will see, we will see." His voice was dry.

"I should think not, Papa. Nevermind thinking about it. This is definite. Tomorrow morning I will be at the mill."

A slight frown puckered Giovanni's brow, but he was too tired to argue and he went to bed.

She knew her father was right. There had never been a woman working in the mill, but the Padrone expected too much from one old man. All that wheat and corn—he could never finish it in time. She was determined that tomorrow she would go to help him.

Another sigh slipped from between her lips. She closed the door behind her and returned to her tiny room. After all, her father was in his late fifties, an old man, others would claim. He was a man accustomed to hard work, but lately, he suffered from erratic health, and she feared all this hard work would cause him harm.

"Foolish old goat," she murmured fondly. Her violet eyes softened as she pushed back a strand of curly hair from her forehead. Sometimes she felt more like a caretaker than a daughter.

After her mother's death, he seemed to be prone to forget about food or time when he was working. If she didn't take him some nourishing food or insisted that he rest, he might have perished from starvation long ago. She was the only person he would allow to bully him into resting. If her father was so determined to finish this work, she would have to help him.

CHAPTER FIFTEEN

Indoctrination

Although these affairs took place numerous years before the Marquis De Sade, they were just as notorious and bizarre—orchestrated orgies. These exercises, it has been rumored through the years, took place in the master bedroom, centuries before, in the room where my mother had given birth to me. The events took place far away from the curious eyes of those unsuspecting relatives and parents of the young women and of their young men.

The few who were aware of these facts respected the Padrone and their religious officials. And, although their own were involved, they were determined that the Padrone and the priest were good men on whom they depended for their food and shelter. They justified their unusual behavior as just suffering from "Libertine Demerit." After all, sex was a natural phenomenon and they were men!

A very few who were aware of the actual facts argued that, after all, Count Lomelleux (the Padrone) had prepared the way for his own behavior. He came from an old noble family in the Province. His taste for luxury and libertinism ate into the family fortune, while his lack of judgment ruined his reputation.

He kept systematically aligning himself with the wrong side in the French Court and had to retire in disgrace. His family, completely up in arms, forced him into army life, where he made a sincere promise of obedience and good behavior to them. In his early army years, he tried to keep to himself, hating every pious man around him, meanwhile suppressing his strong, internal sexual emotions. He prayed constantly to God for help and tried to drown himself in reading religious books to reshape his mixed erroneous sensibility. Life went on dull and unrewarding.

It was not until he reached thirty-five that he had been made Count and sent to be the head of The Castel Du Mont. By this time, he had married an older widow, who asked nothing from him but to be a husband in name only. During the one and only single night of complete drunkenness, he sired a daughter, who turned out to be the only reason his wife was satisfied to live with him. He continued with his numerous, most discreet liaisons with his wife's blessings.

The daughter, unfortunately, had a disfigurement

that ran in his wife's family. She was cross-eyed and there was nothing anyone could do for her. He hated having her grow up like this.

When the boys started calling her, and there were very few, it kind of ruined the girl's confidence from puberty on. Realizing her affliction, she refused to go out and spent most of her time with her mother, or in her room. She knew she only had two choices in life—to marry an old widower or to remain single. She chose the latter for she knew men were only interested in her dowry.

After her mother's death, she took over her mother's household duties. She suspected her father's sexual deviations, but never spoke to anyone about it. It was not the proper thing to do; after all, family was family.

During the nights of indoctrination, she made certain to keep to her bedroom, which was located in the farthest part of The Castel Du Mont. Her father was most thankful for her kind filial understanding and was truly grateful for such a daughter, who, after his departure from this world, would inherit all of his riches.

Although seven years younger, Father Francesco, second in command in the church, had a similar upbringing and was the Padrone's partner in crime. At the age of ten, while living with his mother in Cannes, the only son and inheritor was recalled by his father to

Paris, where he was enrolled in the school of the best and brightest of the upper classes.

At school, the young Francesco learned the pleasures of theatre and also those of flagellation, sodomy and masturbation. In school, whipping was, after all, a noble punishment, and the adults were frequently accused of practicing sodomy, among themselves and with their pupils. Francesco was a very handsome child and an innocent, willing candidate. Hence, he became a lifelong devotee of passive penetration and sadomasochistic scenarios.

After only four years of this schooling, which ended for him at the age of fourteen, he was completely hooked on sex. He woke up every morning looking for pleasure, and when he experienced sex with young women, he was in complete glory. To outsiders he was a complete good-for-nothing, incorrigible individual. His father, now on a trajectory toward an old age of religious contemplation, worried about his son's prospects for marriage, given his rapidly growing reputation. In desperation, he gave his son an ultimatum: he either had to marry an elderly, wealthy widow he had chosen, or join the church. Only then would he inherit the considerable fortune his father was holding.

Two years later, after much soul searching, Francesco found that his father had donated all the money to the church upon his death, with the understanding (by papal decree) that, if his son were to become a man of the church, he would be extended special privileges. And so it came to pass that, through destiny, these two well-versed, corrupt men of faith both found themselves at The Castel Du Mont.

As two comfortable peas in a pod, they gained the villagers' faith and began the town's atrocities in the name of the church. It began with simple ways, such as the Padrone sending some food to the bereaved, who in turn went in person to The Castel with their ever-so-thankful attitude. The Priest, on the other hand, would pay a consoling visit to the very young widows. Being experienced men, they recognized the body language of these innocent, uneducated maidens and acted accordingly (and always in the name of God). Grateful for their services, some of the lonely widows were willing to accept them.

After a while, it was the young virgins for whom they craved, and so they devised "the night-before-the-wedding indoctrination."

The Padrone had now reached the age of fifty, with ugly narrow shoulders, a big belly, scrawny legs matted with black hairs emphasized by silken tight pants, and sneakers of the styles of the day. His body, after so many years of abuse, seemed to be sinking into the sinkhole of evil. His stomach bulged like a swollen bullfrog and he had the puniest of all his manhood. For all his strutting and boasting, after years of over-indulgence, it had been turned into a useless hanging object, no longer able to partake in the usual sexual encounters he had so often enjoyed. His only sex toys, these days, were enjoyable hours of voyeurism. He was now content and received a great deal of satisfaction at being an active and true voyeur.

With the help of Father Francesco and the indoctrination rituals, he was able to enjoy every fantasy he had ever imagined. This ritual, from all accounts, lasted about a dozen years—one of the gloomiest darkest, and most sinful eras of The Castel Du Mont's history.

It was an affair that was whispered about and transmitted verbally, from one generation to another for centuries, but never dared to be written down, until now. NOW IT HAS TO BE TOLD!

CHAPTER SIXTEEN

The Night Before the Wedding

Tomorrow was her wedding day and she was so happy. Clara was so fortunate to have found the most wonderful young man who truly adored her, and he was so good looking, all her friends envied her. From tomorrow on he would be hers, and they would live in the one-room house located just in front of the church, near the back moat where his family had lived.

Both of his parents were now dead. He was an artisan with a piece of land that he cultivated for the Padrone. But he was young and a good worker and, although most of the products went to the Padrone, he was smart and clever enough to keep a good amount for himself. She knew they would never starve as some of the other families did.

She was a bit nervous tonight. This was the last ritual before the wedding. She knew she had to go to The Castel to spend the night for her indoctrination into her religion. Why was she so jittery? Every bride before her had gone, and who believed those silly stories some old women told? They just wanted to scare you.

After all, she was going to her Padrone, who was always so jolly when sharing a few drinks with the men—the Padrone, who took care of them. And her priest, Father Francesco, a handsome and pious man, would be there. All the other girls swooned over him and wished he was a normal single man! He was always so kind and helpful when you went to confession and always seemed to understand your problems.

She had just finished filling the large wooden tub with hot water that her neighbor had lent her for her bath. Someday I will have a large tub of my own, she thought. She scrubbed her skin with the home-made soap and dried herself with the heavy linen towel she had loomed herself as part of her trousseau. She rubbed her skin so hard that it had taken on a very rosy color.

She took her comb and began combing her hair. It was the color of coal, shiny as a pool of ink. "It is your pride and glory," her mother had told her. How wonderful it would have been if her mother and father could share tomorrow's ceremony with her. But her mother had died of smallpox when she had been only ten years old, and her aunt had helped out as well as she could. Her father had died just six months ago as life had finally caught up with him.

She was five feet tall, youthful and blooming with the charm of a bisque doll. She loved her young man, with his broad shoulders, strong honest face and brown eyes, large and shiny with curious liquidity that left her seething with improper thoughts and emotions, which she dared not put to words.

His smile flashed quickly and it was genuine. There was about him a forthrightness—a lack of pretension—she never found in other young men. He had a certain exotic aura. He was marvelous, and tomorrow he would be hers forever and ever. She slowly dressed and set out for the 11:30 p.m. appointment she had at The Castel.

Dante arrived to accompany her. Most people in the village were afraid to enter The Castel, especially at night, but she was not a superstitious person. She had said her prayers and was certain that God would protect her.

Upon arriving in front of the moat, she noticed the bridge had been lowered. Trembling, she kissed her fiancée lightly on the lips, with a promise of seeing him early on the morrow. She bravely walked over the moat bridge and noted that it remained down after she walked over it.

She walked up the marble staircase and pulled the large chain. Old Man Maurizio, the guard-door lackey, answered the door. The guard, it had been told, was deaf. He had long ago saved the Padrone's life in battle and was now permanently set in his employment for life.

He never heard the door bell, but someone had set up waving red ribbons that swayed each time the bell rang and he knew then to open the heavy front door. She entered into the very large kitchen, a room with many ceramic ovens for charcoal. She bet you could cook at least forty dishes at one time.

She followed the guardsman to an upstairs room, and here he left her. This was a warm dark, almost stuffy room, with two windows that overlooked a private churchyard. It was decorated with heavy dark furniture and two large stuffed tapestry-covered couches. For such a small room, they looked out of place. There was a desk by the window with a chair, an oil lamp and papers, and a bookcase on the opposite wall. She did not like this room; she felt she could not breathe easily here.

The door opened and Father Francesco entered, "Good evening child, have you said your prayers and cleansed yourself this evening?" he asked.

"Yes, Father, Cecilia lent me her wooden bathtub, and I prayed for one whole hour. I am ready for God's blessing."

"Then come with me," he replied. Down the long hall they walked, to a large golden leafed door.

He opened the door and she entered. It was a large, spacious room on the second floor of The Castel, with ivory walls and gilded ceilings that had hand-carved and painted frescoes of local flowers and designs.

Unbeknown to her, in one of those large flowers obscured by the dark paint, was a peeping hole, where, on the other side of the wall, comfortably sitting on a lounge, the Padrone could view everything that would go on here.

A superb chandelier dripping with glittering crystal pendants hung from a high ceiling and several candles flickered, making beautiful patterns and rainbow colors all around the room. A rich navy blue carpet around the bed covered part of the white marble floor, and the drapes were of light cerulean blue damask, the color of a sunny sky. A gigantic bed sat in the middle of this room. It was the largest and widest she had ever seen—almost obscene. It looked to her as if it could sleep about six or seven people comfortably.

"Is this not a beautiful room?" asked Father Francesco.

She shyly nodded.

"Well, it's time to begin the indoctrination," he said. "No use wasting any more time."

He was even-eyed and of steady voice, with his words coming with the warm touch of either a great priest or a better actor—a priest feeling so cloaked by blind faith of human nature. A priest, after all was a priest. He promised to keep an eye on all of his parishioners and look over them as a good Catholic. You believed the priest; he was supposed to represent God.

Father Francesco moved slowly toward her with a panther like grace, his dark eyes glittering. Her pulse leaped and her heart was palpitating rapidly. It seemed it would burst at any moment. She tried to speak, but her throat was dry and no words would come. He studied, savoring what he saw, those violet eyes taking in every detail, her hair cascading about her shoulders and her young body, "What a crime to hide such a body like that, with such ugly heavy clothing," he thought. "God made beauty to be savored," he murmured.

"Don't touch me!" she cried.

"Remember, I'm a holy man, a representative of God, and you are here tonight to be indoctrinated properly into your religion, to make you ready to become a good wife to your husband. I'm going to teach you how. I'm going to touch you, oil you all over, as God would, and you are going to love it!"

He reached for the exquisitely beautiful Venetian cut glass urn, poured some aromatic warm oil into his palms and sensually rubbed them together. He stopped, standing very close to her, his hands resting lightly on her thighs. It must be part of the religious indoctrination, very much like the anointing of oil as the priest prepares one when he is about to meet his maker, she thought. But she was scared.

Panic overwhelmed her, and she tried to move past him, toward the door, "I don't want to get married anymore. I don't want to be here. I don't want my religion, I don't want God. I just want to leave now!"

He seized her arm and jerked her toward him. She struggled. He laughed huskily as he wrapped his arm around her. One arm curled tightly around her waist. He lifted her hair and planted his lips on the side of her neck.

Her flesh seemed to burn, "Was this the man that daily listened to everyone's confession, the one that prayed with you when in grief and tried to give solace when a dear one died?"

"I'm going to teach you things, wonderful things, that you will forever thank me for, for the rest of your life. You are going to be a most appreciative student. He turned her around in his arms and then kissed her with lazy deliberation that seemed to cause liquid fire spreading through her veins. He cupped one large hand around her breast, his strong fingers squeezing, kneading—the same fingers that hundreds of times had served the host at Communion.

She hated him for what he was doing to her religious beliefs, and what he was doing to her. She screamed and no one heard. She screamed again, and no one came to help her. All along, she was unaware that behind the wall, the Padrone was in utter ecstasy.

She refused to acknowledge the sensation sweeping over her. She had to stop him. This was all she could think about, she had to stop him.

Certain of victory, he released her. His lips were parted. Heavy lids almost concealed his eyes. In the hazy silver light, his face was all planes and angles, like the statues in the church, deeply shadowed; he was evil but also handsome.

First he ripped her dress off. As she protested he held her arms tightly. He tugged at the straps of her petticoat, so expertly as one who had done this many times before. He began to pull them down ever so slow, revealing more and more firm, round flesh. She was frozen with fear, not understanding what this had to do with church indoctrination. Had all the others before her gone through this?

He was in no hurry at all. After all, he had all night. He seemed to want to savor her each second. He was like a man transported. Nothing existed for him now, but his throbbing manhood and the warm beautiful female flesh that would gratify its quickening demands.

She found herself in a complete state of panic, with mixed feelings against everything she had ever known and been taught. This was the priest she had been told to love and obey. Yet as his hands stroked her breast pressing and probing, they seemed to have a life of their own, swelling under his touch, flesh hardening. She gasped and, against her very own will, a weakness seemed to sweep over her as he bent down to kiss her nipple.

"Remember child this is not me kissing you—it is the kiss of God. Tonight I am God and now, now...." She cried silently. Not being able to accept God in this special manner, she had to stop it now before it would be too late.

He straightened up and made a soft growling noise in his throat and clutching both her breasts in his hands he whispered, "These are the breasts of a Madonna, and like a Madonna...." She pulled back and slapped him hard on the face with all the force she could muster. The sound it made was like an explosion.

He cried out, startled. Her palms stung viciously. She darted toward the door. She did not know where she would go, what she would do, but she knew she had to get out of this room and out of The Castel as soon as possible.

He caught her and grabbed her arm, and swung her violently across the room. She screamed, and he clamped a hand over her mouth, chuckling to himself, not at all angry, but delighted that she intended to put up a fight that would make it all the more interesting.

She wondered how many before her had fought like this and had they won out or had they simply just laid back and given in to his whims?

"So that's the way you want to play it? All right, wench, that's the way we'll play it!" He forced her over to the bed, shoving her down onto the soft mattress. She tried to get up and he shoved her down again, eyes gleaming and lips spreading into a rakish smile. She kicked his shin and he shook his head as if she were a naughty child. He slapped her across the face, his slap even more forceful than hers had been.

Her ears rang and lights seemed to burst inside her head. She fell back sobbing, as he looked down at her with one brow arched high.

"Such games we are going to play, wench, such lovely games."

"No" she cried. "No!" she screamed.

"Scream all you like; no one will hear you or cares." Then he was on top of her. She struggled and he enjoyed that. Smothering her protests with his mouth, he kissed her with a wild abandon that caused every fiber of her being to quicken. He was on his knees now with one leg on either side of her thighs and he was still smiling. He pulled at her skirt, lifted it, exposing her legs. Sobbing, wretched, she tried to throw him off but it was futile. He pulled off his black pants with his one free hand and fumbled with his underwear and then he caught her wrists in both his hands and held her spread eagle beneath him.

"No," she cried. "Please, have pity, no!"

He laughed once more and he loomed over her, a black devil bent on her destruction. She shook her head back and forth, silently pleading. She tried to free her hands, but he held them in brutal grip. Waves of panic rose and crushed over her, and she was trembling all over. "All right, wench, the lesson is about to begin."

He lowered his body over hers, and she cried out as he entered her. He covered her mouth with his hands and tears spilled over her lashes as he drove deeper, with steady deliberation.

She was screaming inside and still fought, struggling beneath him. Then, it seemed the whole world exploded and she went hurting into oblivion, falling, falling, and went completely limp, as senses shattered and nerve ends snapped and life itself seemed to hang suspended in mid-air. She stayed there, afraid to move, peering out of the night's shadows of this ornate room. He was stretched out on the bed, and she could feel him watching her. She never hated one so much in her life and doubted that she ever would again.

He had used her viciously, repeatedly like a whore. He forced her to respond, and she hated him for that most of all. Something inside of her had hardened. She thought of the many women to whom he had done this. How had they reacted? She had heard a few rumors, but this was a powerful, revered holy man, and no one believed the girls' stories.

The priests often reminded the dubious congregation, "Young girls have a large imagination."

Imagination?! This was not an imagination; this was a nightmare.

At that moment she discovered that she had not been aware before, and she promised herself that she would never again be weak and vulnerable. All her illusions and innocence had been shattered. Her father was dead and her fiancée, young and inexperienced. She had no one to turn to who would believe her. And she decided, then and there, that she would do whatever was necessary in order to survive. She felt chilled through and through, and she felt she would never be warm again.

She had heard that one of the women had gone insane and had run screaming up the staircase, so she could throw herself off one of the towers. Others, who did not care, just kept it all to themselves. A few less mature girls told their parents about it, but the priests in church often spoke about the "vivid imaginations of young maidens" and the fathers did not believe their daughters. After all, their own wives had never said any such thing to them. The wives knew, but guarded these pre-marital doings as a great family secret.

To some, in fact, it was probably the best sex they ever had, compared with the inexperienced and primitive sex with their husbands.

Those fathers and fiancées that believed their girls and confronted the holy man and the Padrone, were often convinced after speaking to them, that the Padrone and a man of God would not do this. But others who were more insistent and threatened harm to the priest and the Padrone often were found dead a few days later or just disposed of in some other way. And so, the secret of The Castel continued many years. These were the blackest years of The Castel Du Mont.

Now finished, Father Francesco left the room from a side door, locking it behind him. She took this opportunity to run out the door from which she had originally entered. She ran down the marble staircase, passing the deaf guardsman who by now was sound asleep. She was thankful to find that the moat bridge had been carefully left down and ran across it and away from The Castel.

CHAPTER SEVENTEEN

The Impatient Groom

A faint disembodied noise, like a whisper in an empty room, disturbed him in his sleep. He came awake abruptly and sat up in his feather mattress, with its rope supports squalling. Breathing raggedly, he stared about in the vague glow of the moonlight. Trembling, he called out before he was fully awake, "Clara?"

Waking fully, he realized that whatever startled him from sleep—a witch, a night-sneaking intruder, an unhealthy specter, the devil himself, evil wrath, or beautiful cherubs from the elysian beyond—condemned him to more sleepless dark hours of unabated loneliness in this empty night. He scrubbed his arms against the chill of the strange eeriness infesting his room. He was sad, he was lonely, and he was worried about her. He knew not why. She was with the Padrone and a holy man, so she should be quite safe. His fears, his uncertainty refused to leave him.

She should not have gone. He should have stopped her. The heck with rituals, the hell with religion; they could have run away, far, far away, where no one knew them!

He felt his eyes burn with tears, just like she had cried when he left her last night at the moat bridge of The Castel. Yet he could only lay there, his body fully entwined with fear and apprehension, not wanting to live, not able to die. He choked back a sob of self-pity. He had tried to cry himself to sleep since he had said good-bye to her. He tried to control the painful sobs that wretched his whole body, and sometimes he could stifle those awful heartbroken wails. But, more often, he could not. He lay sobbing in the darkness, wondering if all of the bridegrooms before him had suffered like this. He lay for a long time under his down blanket, which hardly afforded any heat or warmth or relief to his aching heart. Without her tonight, he almost lost the will to live. It did not matter if he died. All that mattered was that she came back safe.

If he lived for anything, it was to touch her hand in his. Her soft kisses would cling to him, showing the depth of the emotion that swelled in their hearts, a sign of shared affection. He was desolate without her. He cursed, voice choked, face pressed into the covers. He listened and waited for a sign he did not find, a face he did not see, a voice he did not hear. Her place was here with him, not in that haunted castle!

No matter how hard he tried, he could not erase this ugliness and horror from his mind. He had to get up and go, to flee, to outrun the agonies that pursued him. He simply could not reconcile, just lying here with self-pity and fear. He dressed swiftly.

The bell tower struck midnight. Mist rose from the river. A solitary man walked along the street on his way to work and stumbled like a sleepwalker towards The Castel, hugging the bag that contained his working tools.

Dante made his way through the dark unlit muddy roads towards The Castel. He sighed heavily in the darkness. He was only twenty-four years old, but had been blessed with extreme natural intelligence. He always seemed to know the correct thing to say at the proper time, and had learned from an early age how to handle those around him.

The Padrone last month had actually approached him with an offer of marriage to his daughter. He had thanked God that he was not a slave, but a free man and was able to humbly refuse. He held his breath. Listening in the darkness, it was as if he could sense the crackling of tension as he suffered through another restless night.

He had arrived at the moat bridge of The Castel, and decided to sit on one of the rocks nearby to wait for his love, no matter how long it would be. He had only been waiting a few minutes, when through the open door his beloved came running.

She ran crying into the arms of her lover. He held her tight and all of his imagined fears must have been so, for in his arms, she shook like a leaf, silent in her grief, unable to mutter a word. He picked her up in his arms and began to carry her toward home.

"No, not your house or mine tonight. Please, let's go to the woods," begged Clara. Fortunately, they remembered the small doorway that led out of the compound to the woods. Through the small secret door that was often left unlocked at night, they made their way out of The Castel Du Mont.

That night they hid in a neighboring cemetery, a place they were certain all were too scared to go. They did not sleep, but talked of what had happened. That night a heavy storm broke, rain beat against the mausoleums and sloshed down the grave stones in torrents. For a while it was impossible to see. He held her tight against him, trying to protect her from this terrible downpour. The storm raged on. By morning they were both trembling from the cold.

Just before dawn they hurried toward the abbey, where the kind nuns, whose nursery school they both had attended, resided. The abbey door was locked as usual. They pulled the chord and the bell rang inside. After a short time, one of the black-gowned pious women answered.

"Heavens, children, what has happened to you?"

"Please, Signora, may we please talk to the mother superior. This is an emergency."

She opened the door wider and led them into the office of Mother Superior, Caterina.

The Mother Superior asked them to sit down and, with her usual stern facial expression, did not reveal any emotions while they were animatedly and emotionally divulging the tale to her.

Though she had heard it several times before, she normally felt helpless to do anything about it except to assist these two unfortunates in the simplest way possible. It was imperative for her to do it without offending the Padrone and the Father, who allowed her to carry out her daily work of taking care of the peasants' children while they worked in the fields. Without her care and establishment, these children would be left alone, as young as they were, to fend for themselves. That she would never allow. She remembered what precious children these two had been when attending her nursery school while their parents slaved at making a living. Somehow, even at the age of four, they seemed inseparable. This must be true love, she thought.

Clara began coughing, and Mother Superior realized the night in the rain was beginning to take its toll. She called one of the sisters and asked her to accompany Clara to one of the empty bedrooms for a warm bath and hot soup. She was to be put to bed immediately.

Dante was given some dry clothes and sent to stay with the monks at the monastery nearby until they could decide what to do. She was furious that such things were allowed to take place under the protection of the government and the church. This time she was determined to do something about it.

The monks were most kind in accepting him for a few nights' stay. He lay in this strange bed, within cold and mute walls that had known only prayers for so many years. In this somber, quiet solitude, his fears, his resentment, seemed to be very strong.

In this rare, private moment, the anger masked something else. He thought of it as a stone in the deep well of his heart, a stone of sadness, of loss that he would never raise into the light for anyone to see, not even his beloved Clara.

She must never find out how devastated he was from the incident. He had to be the strong one. He knew eventually, with his strong love for her, she would heal; but he never would. Had he not been such a devoted Christian, he would have killed the Padrone and Don Francesco with his bare hands.

Instead, for the time being, he just prayed, prayed for God's help. For tomorrow night, he would leave the monastery and make his way back to town to begin his revenge.

CHAPTER EIGHTEEN

The Escape

Dante became gradually aware that his hands and feet were painfully asleep, and then of something, a soggy mass of cloth in his mouth. He coughed and choked and, for a moment, had a frightening belief that he was about to die; but, then the forces of his exertion loosened mucous in his nose, and with effort, he was able to swallow it and breathe enough through one nostril. With a massive effort he forced his lungs full, and then exhaled. More mucous was expelled, but it was a full minute before he had his breath.

He was lying on his side, his hands tied behind him. His upper arms were tied around his chest. His wrists, lashed together, were also tied to his lashed-together feet, which had been drawn up behind him tightly.

He was perched on a rock, just inches from the swift-running river, swollen by the spring ice and melting mountain snow. He tried to roll over on his back ever so carefully so as not to fall off.

The pain, as his arms pulled against the sockets, was excruciating. He was tempted for a moment to just lie there and wait for someone, but he realized his binds were so tight that his circulation had been cut off. If he didn't manage to get free, it was entirely possible that he would lose his hands.

He wiggled and squirmed. He felt pain at the base of his neck that sent a wave of pain down his spine. He heard footsteps. "Lord sweet Jesus," he murmured, "Lord sweet Jesus, someone, please help me!" He opened his eyes and—like a miracle from above—a monk he recognized from the monastery, on his way to working the fields, was bent over him trying to untie the cloth against Dante's mouth.

"You just hold still for a minute, son. I'll have you out of this" and with nimble fingers worked fast and meticulously. Something fell away from his face. Dante pushed at the mask in his mouth with his tongue and it fell out. He was racked by coughing, every cough causing pain in the back of his head and his shoulder sockets.

"Please, friar, cut the ropes free" he finally managed to blurt out."

"I'm working on it, son." All of a sudden his legs were free. He felt the friar working on his wrists. When the pressure of (what he learned a moment later was) rawhide leather thongs was released, he thought he would scream with pain as the blood surged into his hands.

The thongs were cut around his legs. He forced his hands in front of him. They were swollen to twice their normal size and almost black. With an effort of will, he spread his fingers, the pain making him lightheaded, and then made as much of a fist as he could.

"What happened to you, my son? Everything seemed well when you left the abbey last night?"

"I've been attacked, tied and robbed," Dante cried out.

"Do you know who did it?"

"Two burly men accompanied by a well-dressed gentlemen. I could tell this from his clothes."

"Did you recognize them?"

"They were masked but I heard their voices. The two men worked for the Padrone and the gentleman giving the orders was the Padrone! I was beaten, tied and thrown into the river. Those rocks saved me from being carried away by the currents. Last night was a dark night. Without the moon, they could not see that I had not reached the water. One rock I was holding onto fell, and I was able to perch onto another. As the rock fell, it splashed into the water, and they walked away triumphantly."

"That explains it, my son. Can you walk? We must hurry before daylight sets upon us. You must not be seen by anyone. Let them think the river washed you away. Come fast, there are many spies around us."

At the monastery, the head monk listened to the story and a decision was immediately made that both he and the girl must leave at once, for their life was in great danger. A message was sent to the mother superior and within the hour, two nuns walked to the monastery with a basket of fruit and cheese. Only one nun left to go back to the abbey; the other was Clara.

Together they were led to a secret underground passage and with two candles in hand, were instructed to walk deep into the bowels of this dark cave until they reached their destination.

CHAPTER NINETEEN

The Revenge

I t was insane. It seemed to the two lovers that the whole world had gone mad; there was not even time to grieve. They had to think of a plan, a plan to stop those two from harming any more girls—a plan of revenge. They had to rebel even if it meant death to all of them. Death was better than living this way!

The tunnel was long and dreary. When the stale air reached their throats, it gripped it as a thief in the night, choking them slowly. Clara began coughing and Dante handed her his linen handkerchief and instructed her to use it as a mask, tie it around her face and breathe through it, hoping the heavy linen would filter out the humid dank air.

Every now and then they could feel something furry brushing against their ankles. The cave was completely infested with rats. Clara shivered, and Dante tightened his arm about her, in the hope that she would feel completely protected by her man. Poor Dante, today he did not feel like very much of a protector after all that had happened to them. They were now somewhere in this underground fortification tunnel in the deserted depths, which had been built more than a century before by the church's African slave chain gangs. But at the moment they were safe.

Before them was a domed circular space into which the two tunnels converged. They followed the original instructions, to bear left. They could just make out that the other one seemed to be filled or partly filled with a rubble of stones. Perhaps the roof had fallen in.

The left side showed a gaping black mouth and, somewhere in the distance, they heard the soft dripping of water. After twenty yards, they found their feet paddling in an inch or two of thin slime. The water rose slowly as they advanced and soon they stood submerged to their thighs.

Dante bent and tasted it. It was cold, sulfurous and metallic. He surmised that it had to be an underground spring. After about three hours they became very weary, but both refused to stop and rest, afraid that they might be attacked by the rats in the tunnel. They continued, feeling as if they were walking through a nightmare.

They were now walking on sharp dry stones and, finally, when they were certain they could not go another step, they spied a large heavy wooden door. They banged, calling through it, but no answer came. Wearily they kept on banging and, finally, they could hear footsteps approaching. Their mouths went dry. The heavy door opened and Dante smiled at the four friars standing in the doorway.

Later Dante, Clara and the friars set out to see Citizen Baltissera. They tried to stay out of sight, walking not on the roads but through fields. Through the scanty protection of rocks or low hanging tree branches, they came to a farm field. It was midday when they stumbled out of thick trees and saw a village before them. It was scarcely more than a few dilapidated huts, scattered along a dirt track that divided the fields and led to a mound in the distance. On top of the mound rose a fortress. They could see men working in the fields. The nearest house was a bit larger and was set a little apart from the others.

Standing by an open door stood the bulking, aging figure of a man, who long ago had headed an army into Germany. He was a tough soldier, a veteran of many battles. He wore plain leather tunics and heavy boots suited for riding. In spite of his gruff outward look, he smiled. He had a pleasant face. There was such warmth about him, a sense of kind understanding goodness, that Clara, her heart still tormented by what had happened at The Castel, found oddly comforting.

"This is Captain Baldissera. This man can be trusted," noted one of the friars.

They had been walking many hours without food or rest, and weariness so heavy she could not fight it came sweeping through her body, taking away what little strength she had left. She had always been thin, but her lack of appetite during this last miserable week had turned her into just skin and bones. Dante worried about her but now there were other things they had to take care of.

They arrived with a small band of determined rebels at a church just three miles before The Castel Du Mont. Inside, it was dusty and smelled of old incense, mice droppings and decaying plaster. A chicken crooned to itself from the vestry. The evening sun fell through the stained glass window above the altar, luridly lighting the purgatorial flames in which soles struggled lamentably upward toward a pitying but classic Madonna.

They went quickly and carefully around the Stations of the Cross, their feet moving soundlessly over the colored tiles, crossing themselves, genuflecting and clicking off beads of their Rosary as they prayed fast, fervently and with great sincerity.

At the Statue of The Virgin in the west corner, kneeling and with arms stretched wide was a man. "Ave Maria, Piena Di Grazia, Il Signore Teco E Benedetto, E Il Frutto Del Ventro Tuo, Gesu." Then he rose. He crossed himself thrice, kissing his thumb between each complete sign and, reverently, humbly, approached the altar.

Dante approached the altar slowly, inching forward on his knees, praying fervently and rapidly. *"Signore, Dio Santo, Dio Aiutemi Oggi E Per Sempre, Anima Di Fiamma, Espressione Di Eternita, Benedissimi, Aiutami."*

For a long moment, he knelt rigidly upright, his hands crossed against his chest, his eyes wide and slightly glazed, staring fixedly forward, and he kissed the marble altar three times. Only then, trembling with nervous strain, did he rise to his feet to extract the promise candle and place it upon the metal plate along side the altar."

He turned once at the door of the church, glancing up at the aisle to where the pointed flame lifted its gold flower in the dusk and gleamed upon the marble altar. He smiled, suddenly knowing now that everything was going to be all right.

The journey toward The Castel began hours later. They marched through dusty country roads, picking up new members along the way. Finally, they arrived at The Castel. They stormed over the pulled-down moat bridge, as more villagers joined them. The women, old men and children along the way anxiously watched, knowing that something of importance was about to happen.

One group walked straight into The Castel and captured the Padrone. The others stormed into the church where Father Francesco was conducting confession and carried him out by force. The rest of the villagers just stood and watched, knowing well that their day of justice had arrived.

The prisoners were half carried and half pulled through the village streets, demonstrating to all that these sinners had finally been caught and immediately convicted by those who, for so many years, had been the victims of such heinous crimes.

Father Francesco and The Padrone knew that their last hour on this earth had arrived. People threw stones at them, turning both men into bloody, broken creatures. It did not take long for the Padrone to expire, but it wasn't until much later, when the rope around Father Francesco's neck had been tugged tightly several times, harder and harder, that his body gave way; at first into a state of rigidness, followed by complete limpness.

The crowd watching had no tears for the bodies of the bloated Padrone and the handsome priest, now dead and being dragged along cobblestone streets. These foolish, depraved men who had ruled them and ruined them were finally receiving their due punishment.

They were dragged to the middle of the Piazza and hung upside down on two high poles for all to see. The sins of The Castel Du Mont had been vindicated.

The Padrone's daughter, although not directly at fault, was ousted from the village and joined her mother's old relatives in Paris, where she lived a solitary and most disconsolate life.

BOOK THREE

CHAPTER TWENTY

Father Claudio

The sands of time continued to flow. Now, a century after the indoctrination rituals were behind them (but never forgotten), The Castel Du Mont was inhabited by new owners.

Finally, Claudio had been ordained. The cardinal in his home parish had wished him good luck when he had informed him of his new parish. Father Claudio was not a theological disputant or a learned wrangler on Canon Law and did not have a lively admiration for the sound of his own voice box. He was quiet, unobtrusive and sensitive, almost as if he feared someone would find out what was truly inside him. He was a man of humility and had a great deal of respect for human life. He had promised God he would try to dedicate much of his free time to his parishioners.

But where was Father Claudio? The Monsignor's wrath climbed with the rising minute hand as it swept toward eleven o'clock. The clock chimed 10:30 a.m., and a deep burn of irritability reddened his neck. Where was Claudio, his new curate, at such an hour? He had planned on assigning this new priest to the 6:30 a.m. mass tomorrow morning, and Mauro Salussolia was to be his altar boy. Wouldn't you think that a young priest on the eve of celebrating mass in his first parish, would be in his own room on his knees, preparing himself by prayer and meditation?

The clock was chiming the hour when the front door of the rectory opened and the new priest came tiptoeing in. The Monsignor jacked his huge body out of its pastoral armchair and started for the knob of his study door. "Are these your usual hours, Father Claudio?"

A soft answer, thought Claudio, is indicated here. "I'm sorry I am late, Monsignor. I was attending the Ruffo family in prayers. Their two-year-old son was killed today."

"What happened to the child?" the Monsignor inquired.

"Smallpox," answered the priest sadly, "Another life taken." He wondered why.

"I see," answered the Monsignor, "get a good night's rest, Father," he advised. "You're saying your first mass at dawn tomorrow, and nothing gives greater scandal to our savior than the sight of a priest yawning and gawping all over the altar. You get my meaning, Father?"

"Yes, Monsignor, good night," he said before he retired.

Early the next morning, Father Claudio crossed the narrow steps of the stone walk between the parish house and the church, unlocked the door of the sacristy and let himself in. Odors of myrrh and spikenard lay on the almost chilly air. In the ruby flicker of the sacristy lamp, he saw the high broad chest containing the vestments.

Claudio was happy that the sextant, Pinot, had not opened the basement chapel yet, and that the altar boy hadn't yet arrived. The young priest wanted to be alone while he prepared himself for the central act of his being, toward which he moved now with secret exaltation and almost tremulous joy.

He knelt, bowed his head, covered his face with his hands and inwardly supplicated the Divine Father to make him a worthy priest. He washed his hands, layed his biretta on the prie-dieu and approached the vesting bench to attire himself. Taking up the maniple, he kissed the cross in the center and placed it on his left forearm as the symbol of worldly sorrows the priest must bear. Then, taking the stole in his two hands, he said, "Give back unto me, Lord, the stole of immortality, lost by the sins of our first parents."

He was about to place the sacred vestment around his neck when the sacristy door burst open, and the breathless boy rushed past, knocking Father Claudio's biretta to the floor. Picking it up again, he stood panting in the middle of the sacristy floor.

"All right Mauro," said the Father without turning his head, "Get your surplice on."

He hoped this would not be an omen as to how the mass would go. "Hand me my biretta please."

He took the challis in his left hand, placed his right hand over the burse and veil, and held the sacred vessel in front of him, not touching his breast but not far removed from it. Motioning to Mauro to lead off and then falling in behind the boy, Father Claudio walked gravely toward the altar, his mind fixed on the sacred ritual of the mass.

As the mass progressed, he strove to forget all else but the host that he held in his hand. During communion, he placed the sacred wafers on the tongues of the few early communicants. At the conclusion of the mass, he was happy that all had gone well.

The Monsignor thanked him later for the well-directed mass and announced, "Confession, this afternoon. We will start you off with the children. Take the box on the west aisle at 4:00 p.m. and be ready to hear the quaintness that springs 'Oxore Infanitium.'"

A tremor, such as he had never felt before, seized Father Claudio as he opened the door of the confessional and sat down in semi-darkness. He made his final plea to confession of saints and angels. He pushed back the small sliding panel, covered his eyes with his hands, and Father Claudio's work as a loser of sins began.

Through the fine meshed screen came the hasty, almost inaudible murmurs of a twelve-year-old girl. "Bless me father, for I have sinned. It's a week since my last confession, I want to say my penance." Then she poured out a little throat full of venial sins, "I talked in church, three times, and I got angry with my sister when she took my stockings. I slapped my brother once… no, twice. I answered my mother back when she told me to do something, and I was vain in front of the mirror while dressing. For all of these and all the other sins I may have committed, I ask your forgiveness."

What council could be offered this innocent soul? "These little misdeeds of yours are tiny flaws. When The Blessed Mother gazes into the mirror of your heart, will you try not to have even the slightest blemish there?"

"I will try father!"

"For your penance, say three Hail Marys and now make a good act of contrition." He lifted his right hand in the gesture of absolution.

At 6:00 p.m. he emerged from his box, blinking like a mole as he stepped out into the late afternoon sunlight. He then joined Father Antonio, who was pacing up and down in the brick courtyard that butted the castle wall. They had just time for the 6:00 p.m. fast turn before supper.

At 7:30, he was back in his box for the evening stint. The first half dozen penitents were pious, married women, who repeated on a slightly more adult level, the trivial offenses of their children. "I gossiped twice; I envied my neighbor; I was late for Mass; I ate meat on Friday because I was out of eggs and cheese; I refused my wifely duty to my husband on two separate occasions because...."

He found that women were more likely to exaggerate their offenses than the men. The men would come right out with it—"I committed adultery four times." He was beginning to feel complacent about his handling of things in general. Until, as he opened the slide to his left, a faint odor of perfume, vaguely carnation, struck his nostrils. The delicate voice of a young woman began a pianissimo recital of the usual minor offenses, a trifle sulky. After the briefest hesitations, she said, with neither shame nor pride, "During the past six months, I've had sexual relations, with a man, many times." He asked the natural question, "Why don't you get married?"

"He's married."

"Does he want to marry you?"

"I've begged him to leave his wife and marry me, but he said he can't, because of the children."

"Will you continue to go with him?"

"Yes, Father. I love him very much." Then, the fabric of her stubbornness gave away and she uttered a miserable, "What shall I do?"

"Hard though it is, you must break with this man. There is no other way to lasting happiness for the two of you if you continue as you are now. You are greatly sinning and you must stop this business of illicit relations. It is dangerous, immoral and cheap. Do you intend to stop?"

The girl shook her head, "I can't."

"In that case, it is not within my power to grant you absolution. You cannot receive the sacrament of penance until you have made a firm resolution to give up your simple way of life."

The girl rose from her knees, "Why did I come here anyway? I might have known," she murmured angrily. Leaving a scent of carnation behind her, she flew from the confessional.

His instinct was to run after her, beg her to be patient with the church and himself. But he could do none of these things. He knew he had been technically correct, refusing absolution; but he knew also that he had been too brusque, too unbending, and not tactful enough. His want of skill had caused a troubled soul to slip through his fingers. He hoped to do better.

Claudio stepped out on his ceaseless round of

parish duties to the sick and the housebound. He brought the Eucharist in its golden pys and, on many a night of fallen snow, he carried the case of Holy Oil down streets covered with heavy, almost impassable snow to anoint the eyes, lips and limbs of the dying—sheer routine most of it.

Fiorina, loveliest of the Benvenuti clan, walked nervously to a secluded part of the cemetery to meet her sweetheart, whom she was not allowed to invite to her home. Then, a good-looking boy stepped out from behind a gravestone and said, "Cara Mia, I thought you'd never get here!" Thereupon, he took her arm and led her to a still more secluded part of the cemetery where they sat on the grassy knoll, talked and kissed again till dark. They knew the gatekeeper would lock the front gate at five o'clock, but they were in love and they were young, and they could later climb out over the high fence. In the meantime, they enjoyed these stolen moments in complete privacy. They kissed and hugged and kissed some more.

"Love is so grand when one is young and foolish!"

CHAPTER TWENTY-ONE

Monsignor

Next day in church Father Claudio noticed hallowed-eyed Cornelia kneeling at the Shrine of the Virgin, her eyes fixed on the lily-fringed heart of the Madonna, as she lighted a candle for the speedy recovery of her sweetheart, Victtorio Porelli. If Victtorio hadn't been stabbed twenty four hours ago in a knife fight, he would have married her this day. Now three months pregnant, Cornelia wept natural tears and beseeched a miracle.

"Let my Victtorio live, Madonna of Sorrows. Stop the blood coming from his mouth and I will make you a perpetual Novena of my life." She lifted her eyes to Mary's Statue and screamed as she saw blood dripping from the Madonna's flowered crowned heart.

The Monsignor unloosened the three center buttons of his cassock, stretched his large legs under the rolled topped desk in his room, and lighted his evening cigar. His favorite dinner of barley soup, roast beef and boiled potatoes lay just behind him, and an evening of "Counting Up," the happiest time of the week, lay just ahead. In the top drawer of his desk were three canvas bags, the first, with the coins collected at the 9, 10, and 11 o'clock masses that Sunday. The second held miscellaneous coins—mostly pennies—taken that week from the poor boxes and the votive candle offerings. The third and the most valuable, was the one the Duchess donated weekly. He added up the jottings. There were one hundred and twenty liras, a creditable sum. After deducting the liras he must forward to the diocesan treasury, there would still be some left to carry on the work of his parish.

Outside his window rose the clatter of voices, shrill and loud. He glanced at his watch, 9:45 p.m. What tumult was going on at this hour? He flung up his window and saw a throng of people mulling about in the brick and stone areaway at the entrance to the church.

Father Claudio, white-faced, abruptly opened the door. He explained that they were saying they had seen a miracle. "Monsignor, some girl came in here this afternoon and lit a candle in front of The Blessed Mother. Then she went home and found that her boyfriend, good as dead from a stiletto stab, was sitting up in bed, asking for polenta. These people have been flocking up in droves here ever since!"

A woman pushed open the door, dashed into the room, "My baby has been vomiting for the last three days" she cried. "The Blessed Madonna will make him keep his milk." A large crowd had formed behind her and they were beginning to push forward.

Father Claudio cried, "Children of the miraculous queen of heaven, listen to your priest. Turn around and let me through and follow me in the spirit of orderly devotion. I will lead you to the feet of the Madonna."

Into the dimly lighted church, down the side aisle, buzzing like excited hornets, they approached the triple tier of candles, glazing in fiery apostrophes before the little niche that sheltered the figure of The Virgin. Kneeling at the shrine, he gazed upward at the statue. Blood red drops falling from The Virgin's heart were splashing in a tiny pool at the base of the statue.

"If I could only dip my finger into that stuff," thought Father Claudio. But a buzz-like flight of asthmatic hornets rose behind him. "No time for scrutiny now."

Emotions were bubbling dangerously. He must drain them somehow. But how? By prayer? What prayer should we say? Say the Rosary of course. He turned to the people.

"This is the first Sunday of this month," he said, "the month of Mary Song." The feeble wail of a retching baby was the only sound in the church. "Let us garland her with flowers, the flowers of the five glorious mysteries of The Holy Rosary."

The Monsignor stormed into the church to find out for himself what was going on. He saw a field of bent heads and heard Father Claudio's clear voice uttering the first part of the Angelical salutation, "Hail Mary, full of grace. . ."

He tiptoed out of the church. "He might be a new priest, but he certainly has a way with people," he murmured.

They said The Rosary five times before the crowd was completely calm. Meanwhile, the drops continued to fall. There was awe in the eyes of the people as they filed singly past The Virgin Statue on their way out. The last to leave was the woman with the retching baby. "Look" she said, with peace in her voice and eyes. "He has not thrown up since The Rosary began."

It was 1:00 a.m. before the church was empty. "Now," said Father Claudio, "We will see what goes on." He opened the gate before The Virgin's Shrine, came closer to the Statue and reached out to touch the crimson heart with his finger. As he did so, a soft red drop fell on his fingernail. He looked upward into the ceiling shadows high above the Virgin's Head.

Rusty water falling from a crack in the ceiling, was leaking down, a drop at a time, onto the heart of Mary! It struck the cheap brilliant color in a solvent splash and continued falling to the floor. The miracle of the leaking ceiling was plastered the next morning under the sound of hammers and plaster.

The mystical music died, but its echo lingered on. It lingered in the heart of Cornelia. She was married to her Victtorio a few days later at a nuptial mass, celebrated by Father Claudio.

It lingered in the heart of the shawled woman, whose baby died of an intestinal obstruction; and, especially, it lingered in the memory of Father Claudio, and with the Monsignor, who never forgot it.

"I've got myself a curate! At least one who knows how to get along with these people," the Monsignor chuckled to himself.

Having gotten himself a curate, he now proceeded to put him to work. There was plenty for Father Claudio to do. With his priesthood honing in him like a trident, he waded chin deep into parish waters. He celebrated mass daily, alternating with Father Antonio at the 6:30 a.m. service. He baptized babies and was quite expert at soothing their shrieks after the Holy Water had been poured over their soft pink heads. On three evenings a week he stood house watch, patiently listening to the troubles of garrulous old women who came to have a medal blessed, and then launched forth with the unsolicited details of their lives. Getting them out the front door, with their tales still in the telling was a triumph of tact. Observing his manner with these old biddies, the Monsignor promptly made Father Claudio his spiritual advisor.

CHAPTER TWENTY-TWO

Roxanne (The Birth)

The village women, all perfectly silent, stood about the bed watching what was happening there with tense anxious faces. Sympathy, anguish, pity, and apprehension were expressions they showed, as their eyes shifted from the tiny red baby lying beside the woman who had just given birth to the sweating midwife bending down and working with her hands beneath the spread blankets. One of the women, pregnant herself, bent over the child, her eyes frightened. Then, all at once, the baby gasped, gave a sneeze and, opening its mouth, began to yell. The women sighed with relief. As the midwife went to the fireplace and sat down to bathe the child from a basin full of warm red wine, the pregnant woman slid her hands beneath the blankets and, with firm gentle movements, began to knead the mother's abdomen.

There was a look of strained anxiety on her face that amounted almost to horror, but it vanished swiftly as the woman on the bed, slowly opened her eyes and looked at her. Her face was drawn and haggard with the strange new gauntlets of prolonged suffering, and her eyes lay sunk in dark sockets. Only her light blonde hair flung in a rumpled mass about her head, seemingly still alive. Her voice was thin and flat, scarcely above a whisper. "Is that my baby crying?"

"Yes, that's your baby daughter!" The baby's angry sounding squalls filled the room.

"But I wanted a boy!" Tears filled her eyes and ran from the corners streaking across the temples. Her head turned away wearily as if to escape the sound of the baby's cries. A kind of dreamy relaxation was beginning to flow over her. It was something almost pleasant, and as it took hold of her more and more slightly, dragging at her mind and body, it seemed to offer release from the agony of the past three days. She could feel the quick light beating on her heart. Now, she was being sucked down into a whirlpool, then swirled up at an ever increasing speed. As she spun. she seemed lifted out of herself and out of the room, swept along in time and space. She was beginning to move restlessly, conscious of painful cramps in the muscles of her arms and legs. She could see only dimly now as if she had her eyes under water. Although she could not tell how much time had gone by, the woman was still working on kneading her belly with capable strong fingers, her face strained and wet.

She became aware of the other women nearby, of a bustle and stirs in the room, and now, one bent down to lay a warm cloth across her forehead, at the time removing another which had grown cool. Blankets had been piled on her, but still her face was cold and wet; and she could feel moisture on her fingers. Her ears were ringing and the feeling of dizziness came again, swooping down and then whirling her up and away until she saw nothing but a hazy blur. She heard only a confused murmured babble. Then she moved slightly, trying to ease the cramps that knotted again and again in her legs. Very slowly and with great effort, she drew her hand from where it lay at her side under the blankets and raised it toward her. As she did so, she saw that the palm and fingers were smeared with wet blood. For a moment, she stared at it dreamily, without comprehension, and then, all at once she understood why she had such a strange sense of comfort, as though she lay in a warm bath. Her eyes widened with horror and she gave a sharp cry of pleading and protest.

"Please help me, I don't want to die!" The other women were sobbing widely.

"I can't be dying," she thought," I don't want to die, I want to live!"

She tried to speak again, to beg for help, to demand it, "Don't let me die." But she heard no words. She could not even tell if her lips formed them. And, then she slowly began to drift, floating back into some warm pleasant world, where there was no fear of death. She drifted willingly and welcomed this promise of relief. And then, all at once, she could hear again, loud and clear, the sound of her daughter's cries. They were repeated over and over but grew steadily fainter, fading away until, at last she heard them no more.

The baby was christened Roxanne.

CHAPTER TWENTY-THREE

Roxanne's Saga

Hers was a familiar story. Pale and shaken, the girl descended her father's stairs, clutching a pathetically battered bag and trying not to sob. Her cheeks were stained with tears, and her blue velvet eyes filled with a miserable resignation. Roxanne was only fifteen years old. She had come to Paris only a few months ago from the country where she had been raised by kind friends after her mother's death. They could no longer afford to keep her.

She had not been a happy child. They had tried to be kind to her, but they had twelve other children to feed, so she was always the last for anything. They had told her that she was a bastard of an aristocratic lord. She had her father's cool patrician good looks and her mother's high color and earthy allure. The combination was as unusual as it was striking. She was slight and slim and unbelievably beautiful. She certainly must have had aristocratic blood in her veins, for she was different, unlike the other robust, rosy-cheeked lasses who were typical of the thousands of girls who poured into Paris to go into service. She had now been dismissed without references, and she had no hope of finding another post.

The lord stood in the lower hall, vainly and with tight lips of anger, watching the girl he could not force or conquer. She moved slowly toward the front door defiantly, for none of the servants ever used the main entrance.

Count De La Manse arched one dark eyebrow in puzzlement and disappointment for not having mounted this filly, but he made no effort to stop her. The girl paused and, for a moment, it looked as though she might burst into tears and plead, begging him to let her keep her job as a scullery maid. He waited and frowned with excitement, drawing himself up in amusement. Roxanne looked at him with her sad velvet eyes, but she didn't plead. She simply looked at him hopelessly, wretched, and then opened the front door and stepped outside. She had some education but no money and no hope of surviving unless she joined the pitiful parade of prostitutes who swarmed over Paris by the thousands. Distraught, she stepped out into the street and wished she were older, plainer, paler and unappealing. She had never been vain, but knew she was an attractive girl. In her village, the young men had been after her ever since she had been twelve. As an orphan she was a natural prey, she recalled. But she had ignored their crude invitations and eluded their clumsy caresses. For a short while she had been privileged to attend a refined expensive school for young ladies that was paid for by the lord of the township, "for the crowned beauty queen," a title she had won three years in a row.

The other young girls in school had resented her because of her rich, coal black hair, her high sculptured cheek bones and her slender body that was undeniably shapely. She loved school and was a bright student. She was always eager to learn and, if the other children shunned her because of her bastardry and frequently taunted her, she tried not to let it bother her. Although she wore her hair in a severe coronet of braids on top of her head, she couldn't conceal its rich luster, a vivid combination of black and strong moonlit highlights. Her plain brown dress had severe long sleeves and was high necked. But somehow, that only emphasized her full breast and narrow waist. She was the kind of female men always pursued.

She had grown up since then and she knew now who she was—the bastard daughter of an illiterate barmaid and a pier of the realm. She belonged to neither her world nor his. She had never experienced her father's way of life, and the special school training she had received had made it impossible for her to go into her mother's lifestyle. She had come to Paris, naively believing she could put her education to good use. Her education didn't matter, her wits did. In order to survive, she would have to use them in every turn, for it was a hard, cruel, unfeeling world for a young woman alone.

Count De LaManse, in his abuse and having fired her for not succumbing to his wants, had shattered her illusions. But unknowingly, he had given her the determination she needed to forge ahead. Others before her would probably be dead from starvation or venereal disease before the year was out. But that wasn't going to happen to her. She would never again be dependent solely on what others were willing to allow her. She had been walking about Paris for two days now, trying to find a job, but none were to be had. She was very tired, but had to go on. She could not give up.

She heard the distant rumble of thunder. The sky was a dark slate gray, filled with ponderous black clouds that seemed to drop a sinister purple light. The alley she was walking through was littered with fruit rinds, paper and rotting debris, and the row of flimsy brown wooden hovels seemed to keep together to keep from collapsing.

Something long and furry scurried among the debris. A cat perched on one of the window sills let out a loud howl and pounced, catching the rat between its jaws and dashing down the alley with it. She shuddered. An aged, grotesque, obese old woman in a filthy blue dress and tattered black shawl staggered into view, clutching an almost empty bottle of brandy. Glancing at Roxanne as she passed, the old woman grinned a toothless grin and waved. Roxanne could hear the old woman crackling with delight that someone else was as desperate as she was, and shuffled through the squalid alley with a few drops of liquor left in the begrimed bottle.

Roxanne was hungry and began feeling weak in the knees. A cloud of black wings rushed over her, closing everything else out. Someone behind her rushed over, and a strong arm seized her before she could fall. He held her tightly; and, gradually, the wings vanished. She was in a state of shock and, through the mist, she could see the man who had just saved her.

"Easy, milady, everything will be all right." The rest of his words seemed to fade away, and the next thing she knew, she was in a carriage riding to where she knew not. The carriage stopped in front of "The Maison Bois Verde residence, and the coachman carried her into the house. He was met by the lord of the house, who had a puzzled look upon his face. "What is this, Raymond, he asked?"

"I beg your pardon, sir. I found this lady in a faint and was taking her to the housekeeper for some help." The Lord looked at this hopeless but beautiful child-woman and wondered about her. "Yes, Raymond, you have my permission. Go along now!"

The dowager, Countess Du Pons, always awakened early in the morning, and decided to join Matilde in the kitchen for her first cup of coffee. Matilde, the cook, was busy setting up a breakfast tray as she entered. "My son is up already?" The Countess asked in surprise.

"No, madam, this tray is for the poor starving young lady the coachman found fainting in the streets last night. The Count gave his permission to feed her, clean her up and send her to bed."

"Did my son see this lady?" she asked.

"No, I don't believe so. He just seemed to feel sorry for her. I put her in the empty room in the servant's wing."

"Thank you, Matilde. I think I'll take a look at her. It will give me something to do." Slowly she walked up the servant's backstairs to the third floor of the dwelling, reminding her of her days working as a servant, ages and ages ago. No one had ever known her secret; but she always had a soft heart for all her workers.

Roxanne sat up as the Countess walked in, frightened to utter a word, for fear of immediate expulsion from this comfortable room. "Why, you are just a child, my dear!" the Countess observed and touching her forehead, continued, "You also have a fever." Matilde entered with a breakfast tray.

"Eat child," the Countess ordered. "And, after her breakfast, help her to one of the bedrooms in the main house and call the doctor to see what is causing her fever." She patted Roxanne on the wrist and left.

The Countess was a true grand dame, a most distinguished eighty-year-old matron. She had lived a long time and buried three husbands, and she loved her only son very dearly. She strongly wished he would soon wed a young wife and give her grandchildren, before her almost-finished life would be over.

Later she joined the Count Du Pons at breakfast. "Forgive me, Mother. I did not hear you come in. Please do sit down and join me for breakfast," he said. She smiled and, as the butler pulled her chair out, she sat down and began drinking her second cup of coffee of the day.

"Mother, last evening, I gave permission to the servants to take in a lost, starving, pathetic, young lady that the coachman found almost fainted away. He asked me to give her lodging for the night. She looked so weak and forlorn, I felt sorry for her, just as you do with stray kittens!"

"I know son. I met her this morning and had her moved to one of the bedrooms upstairs, where she would be more comfortable. She did seem like a poor innocent waif. She was running some fever, and I had the servants call the doctor. He is due at any minute."

"Mother, you are always so sweet, kind and caring."

"Actually, this will give me something to do. It's been difficult for me to pass my time away now that my eyes no longer can see to work my quick-point embroidery. I used to love it so much!"

"She might be able to be good company for you for a few days, Mother."

"Madam, the doctor has arrived," the butler announced. "Thank you, Renauld. Please take him upstairs, I will speak to him after the examination."

As they finished breakfast, the doctor was descending the staircase. "Renauld, do pull up a chair for the kind doctor, so he can join us for breakfast."

"Thank you, Countess Du Pons. I'd be honored," the doctor happily answered.

"And what about the girl?" asked the Count.

"She seems very run down," replied the doctor, "suffering mostly from malnutrition. One month of a good home would set her right back on her feet. But, of course, where can she find someone willing to take her in for a month?"

After breakfast, the doctor thanked the Du Pons for their kind hospitality and, with a great deep bow of gratitude, left to make more calls.

CHAPTER TWENTY-FOUR

La Mason De Les Bois Verde

Roxanne finished that wonderful breakfast. Oh! How wonderful it was to be here in this mansion. The air was heavy with the fire burning brightly in the fireplace. This was the first time she had slept in a room with a fireplace of her own. What luxury! The air felt hot with her heavy clothes. The sheet felt damp, and she thrust its cleanliness away like a sweaty embrace of some unwelcome suitor.

Hearing a soft knock at the door, she sat up as the Count entered her room. She looked so small in such a big bed that it made him smile with a paternal look. She looked at him with eyes full of fear, as men had never been kind to her. She knew she could not give way to fear. It would be all too easy to succumb to the panic inside. She smiled shyly. "What a stoic and perky young lady you are." the Count noted. "Relax. Mother has made up her mind to get you back to good health. You are in very good hands!"

"But I have no money to repay you," she uttered.

"Don't worry about it now. Just rest and get well." Without any further words, he turned around and walked out. No one but the servants visited her that first day. She ate the meals the maid served her and simply enjoyed the luxury of this wonderful room.

The doctor had told her that she must rest and try to sleep as much as she could so she would be able to regain her good health. Sleep was not within her grasp, however. In the darkened, curtained room, she lit a candle, setting it aglow before placing it on the night table. Restlessly she paced about the room. What was she doing here? What did this family want from her? Why were they being so kind? No one before had been so nice to her without wanting something in return.

She spent two heavenly weeks at this glorious mansion, rested and ate very well. The doctor declared her "fit as a fiddle," and she felt wonderful. Her only chores were to read to the Countess whenever she requested and to sit each day for tea and "chat a while." The Countess was elated for the companionship of this young woman, and she found her to be extremely intelligent and a fast learner. She read the stories so well that the Countess could actually picture herself as part of them.

CHAPTER TWENTY-FIVE

A Blossoming Love

The Count, although a mature man of forty-nine, was beginning to be quite smitten with this young woman. She seemed to bring out those long forgotten deep feelings he had, and began wishing he were young again. It was wonderful! He enjoyed her company and found himself quite disturbed at the time she spent with his mother, almost as if he were in competition for her attention, wanting it all for himself. And, as a faithful lover, he even went as far as to cease his daily visits to the ladies that had fulfilled his needs for so many years.

To his surprise, he had become truly celibate these last few weeks. His happiest moments were those he spent with her, talking and, what seemed, innocently flirting. He would tease her about the many young men she must have met, and with how many had she bedded?

And with those wide velvet eyes, she would innocently reply "Dear sir, when I give myself to a man, 'twill be under the vows of matrimony, with all the love I can muster. Sir, I have a dream of the perfect wife whose only purpose in life is to make her husband happy. For days I walked the streets, ignoring those about me and their rude remarks. I ate nothing and that's how I came to faint in your coachman's arms. I will never allow any man to take advantage of me. If I fall in love, then, and only then, will I give myself in marriage. And as soon as I can get a job, I swear, I will repay you for your kindness. In the meantime, you should not speak to me this way."

"Rest assured, madam, I did not invite you here to warm my bed. It was a gesture very much as one would take with a starving kitten."

"So I am just a starving kitten!" she snapped back, forgetting she was speaking to someone quite above her rank. This brought a smile to his usually serious face. "My, this one is not only intelligent but has some spunk." She will make it all right! he thought.

"Fear not," he continued, "I have all the wenches I could possibly want. I take enjoyment in teasing you, for you are different from the others and mysteriously fascinating to me. So, relax and enjoy a bit of the good life, my dear. From you I ask nothing." He could not understand why he was explaining—almost apologizing—to the young waif. After all, she meant nothing to him and would be gone to her destiny in a couple of days.

"I suppose I should feel grateful, sir!" she murmured softly. "I do get this way when men try to pry into my business. I never seem to be able to trust any of them and always wonder what they want from me."

"Oh yes, my dear, one can plainly see that you have a body designed by the devil and eyes like velvet fire, perfect for falling in love with. I personally have not been in love since earlier years, but somehow, you intrigue me. And with all of my daily duties keeping me busy most of the time, I feel I am entitled to some innocent diversion.

"Mother and I have enjoyed your refreshing company. So, forgive me if I get a bit abrupt. I am not accustomed to the feelings of young maidens. The time is late. Go and get your rest."

She went to her room, undressed, washed and changed into a clean nightgown, given to her by the Countess. She was so excited by the conversation she just had with the Count that she knew it would be impossible to sleep. She stretched out on the bed and watched the darkness of the night stealing into the room through the open windows. She closed her eyes puzzled, worried about her future, yet feeling some happiness for having found, even for just a few days, such comfort. Then, she seemed to sink into a nest of heavy darkness, floating through the shadows.

When she opened her eyes, the room was filled with a heavy violet mist. The curtains billowed softly as cool breezes drifted in from outside. Alarmed, she sat up, realizing that she must have slept for hours. The sun was already up and the last vestiges of darkness had turned into light. She brushed her hair and slipped into her dress, just in time to join the Count at breakfast. He seemed pensive this morning and she ate in silence in fear she might disturb him in his deep thoughts.

The Count, to his dismay, found himself falling madly in love with this beautiful young maiden. He enjoyed watching her every graceful movement and the innocent manner she had when she shook her head back when she laughed. He was much fascinated and completely lost in her femininity.

She could not guess the depth of torture she put him through, for beneath his silken taunts, he burned with consuming desire for her. At night he tossed sleepless upon his oversized canopy bed, while visions of her flitted around him.

Roxanne was soft and beautiful, lovely and tempting across the table. He was ever conscious of her. He began turning hopes of possessing her, but marriage was a different thing. He had been married once before. The marriage had ended when his young wife died giving birth to his stillborn son. Here was Roxanne, trim, tiny and fragile, like a budding rose ready to be plucked, yet young enough to be his daughter.

The scent of her lingered in his mind, the scent of exotic blossoms crushed on satin skin and beneath it the sweet smell of women mingled with a twinge of soap. He felt fire burning in his blood and he could find no way to quench it, for the thought of another woman soured in his mind when he compared them to her. He realized that he had to have her. He must speak to mother today.

He smiled that satisfying smile of a man who had reached a worrisome decision. And Roxanne smiled back, and returned to her breakfast.

"Will the Countess be coming down this morning?" she asked

"No, Roxanne" he replied, "She is feeling a bit under the weather, but asked if you would join her in her bedroom for some reading after breakfast."

"Oh, yes, of course I will," she said and stood up to leave. "Finish your breakfast first; the reading will wait," he commanded. Roxanne sat and finished her breakfast.

CHAPTER TWENTY-SIX

The Annunciation

He could wait no longer. Leaving the breakfast table before he even finished, he excused himself to Roxanne and rushed to his mother's room. By the serious look upon his face the duchess knew it had to be something urgent.

"Mother, I have fallen madly in love with Roxanne. Her beauty dims the very radiance of this heaven. You know I have not yearned for anyone since Clothilde's death and have been a very lonely man. This young girl has made me feel alive once more. It's as if my life depended on her, Mother. I love her so very dearly and would like to make her my wife as soon as possible."

His mother hesitated for a moment. She had guessed long ago about this May-December infatuation and wondered if his decision of marriage was a sane one.

She was a sweet thing, this Roxanne, but they hardly knew her. Position meant nothing to her. Was she not a governess when the Count, her first husband, had married her? And she had made a darn good wife. But Roxanne was so young and inexperienced and needed much grooming before being presented to their society. Yet, with some work it could be done.

"This girl seems superior to the wanton women in our circles who have been buzzing around you for years. After all, you are a man and need a woman to take care of you when I am gone. You can't expect me to live forever. She seems sweet and intelligent enough. But what do you really know about her?" she asked.

"Mother, please," he pleaded, "Do not be too critical of her. I know all I need to know. In my aging heart, I'm certain she is the one for me."

"All right then, son. We will employ Monsieur Mellon and he will spend the next two grueling months tutoring her in the ways of becoming a fine lady of our class."

It was time to speak to Roxanne. He had to ask her to marry him. Could she possibly refuse him? That afternoon he met her in the library, where she was quietly sitting reading the book, *Ivanhoe*. He sat down next to her and asked if she was enjoying her stay at Les Bois Verde.

"Oh, how can you ask me this? I don't know if I will ever be as happy as I have been these last two months" she sighed.

"How would you like to live here for the rest of your life?"

"Me? Has your highness gone balmy? Are you offering me a job as a companion to the Countess?" she asked apprehensibly.

"No, Roxanne, not as a companion,"he replied. She sighed forlornly.

"Am I to be tortured more than ever, Roxanne? Don't you know that the merest sight of you is enough to bring me pain?" His voice was low and husky in her ears, and he had to dip deeply into her reservoir of will to dispel the slow numbing of her defenses. "Do you know, Roxanne, how my arms ache to be filled with you? To be so near and never touching is agony for me." His fingers lightly stroked between her shoulder blades. "Are you some dark witch to bring me Hell on earth—being that which I desire most and that which I may have least of? Be soft Roxanne, be woman, be my love and be my wife." He bent closer, his lips drawing perilously near.

"Your highness," Roxanne spoke sharply and, jerking away from him, commanded to behave. "I will not argue or fight you, for I should be forever thankful to you and the Countess' kindness, but I refuse to succumb to any man's desire."

"My love, I am a man, you are a woman. How else should I behave?"

Her glance flitted hesitantly across his beautiful silk garments before her eyes lifted to meet that steady predatory stare. Suddenly, Roxanne felt like a hen before a wily fox, expecting to be devoured at any moment. She brushed away his hand as he reached to caress her hair. "But Roxanne, I am asking you to be my wife."

"Oh lord, you are, you truly are?"

"Yes, Roxanne, and what is your answer?"

"Yes! Yes! Yes." She roared with great delight.

"Do not fear my love. Tomorrow Monsieur Mellon will introduce you to all the rules and regulations required for being a true lady and in no time at all, no one will know you had not acquired these from birth."

And on the morrow, her concentrated studies began. In two months, she emerged the most beautiful butterfly, followed by a most successful coming- out party. Paris was at her feet. Everyone came to congratulate the Count in choosing such a prize. The wedding was the major event of the year. Festivities over, they retired to the bedroom. She was timid, apprehensive, afraid of this man—the man she had promised to love and obey in sickness and in health for the rest of her life. Her heart quickened with anxiety as he entered the room. This was her wedding night and she was frightened. Never having had a mother to guide her, she did not know what to expect, or how to act as a bride.

A soft light shone from a far-away candle, set on a small table on the desk, and it lined her profile in radiance that made her warm and angelic. His eyes touched the hair that tumbled, in black highlighted curls, cascading down her back. Just to stand near to her was a heavy wine!

He saw the arch of her brow, which he had longed to caress with his own since they met. He loved the firm but gentle thrust of her jaw and the slim white column of her throat where her hair fell away, baring its ivory softness. His own blood thudded in his ears and his feet seemed to move of their own volition until he stood close to her by the bed.

Roxanne could feel his nearness in every fiber of her being. The manly odors of leather and horses invaded her senses. Her pulse raced and her heart took flight. He was a rich man with a title, and she finally had succeeded in becoming his wife with the title of Countess. The dream she had wished for so many years! She wanted to say something, yet it was as if she was frozen and could only wait for his touch. His hand moved forward and his fingertips touched her hair.

He slowly lowered himself into bed. She instinctively moved away with fear. "What's the matter, dear wife? Why would you be afraid of me, of fulfilling your marriage vows? Am I something less than human? Why do you want to deny me that is what is mine?"

He then remembered she was a virgin, unlike the women he had often used these last twenty-some years.

He lowered his face until he stared into hers. His eyes were bright with his own frustration and hunger. He was feeling like a twenty year old, full of passion and abandonment.

"You are my wife now, in name as well as in action, and I shall make you mine forever. Relax now. I shall not hurt you."

Roxanne began to struggle and he clasped his arms about her holding her close, smothering her movements in an embrace of steel. Sobbing, Roxanne pushed in vain against his chest. Her head tipped backwards with her effort, and his mouth crushed down upon hers.

In the way of love, fear was transformed into passion as her arms slipped upward about his neck and were locked in frantic embrace. His lips twisted against hers and the full heat of his hunger flooded him until his mind reeled with the frenzy of her answer. He had expected a fight and, instead, found the fury of consuming desire trembling sweet on her lips, her mouth stirring at the quick thrust of his tongue meeting hers. It was the bliss of the nuptial night, the thunder of passion, the sweetness of spring awakening, the urge of surrender. All merged into one, and mingled into the mutual rhythmic movements of their bodies as she took him into hers. A trickle of blood formed on the sheets and she gasped with pain, but the blend was explosive, fusing them with oneness and flinging them into a plunging flight until it left them breathless and exhausted in the afterglow.

There was a long silence. "Your highness," she whispered. "Yes, my love, aye" the answer was soft as his lips touched her brow. "Yes my little Countess."

"Is this what love and marriage is all about?" she asked. "Yes, my dearest, and much more." More, what more could there be? A hint of passion accompanied by so much pain and humiliation—is this the payment she had to submit to for title and riches? Roxanne quietly sobbed and, at this moment, was not too certain as to who received the best of the bargain.

And, so, she settled into the role of a married woman. Her aim was to please her husband's every need, but often lately, he objected to other men paying her attention or even just looking at her. He argued constantly as a jealous lover, and picked on her constantly.

"I cannot stand those floppish manners of the men in court," he would complain, but in more truthfulness, he admitted hoarsely, "I can't bear one fondling or ogling. The golden flame of his eyes touched her with fury. "That privilege, madam, I claim is mine and mine alone."

"And so you do, sir," she replied, teasing him ever so skillfully, but this did not quiet him.

"You don't know how clever they are, madam, now that mother is gone, and I am attending business every day. These rascals could easily seduce an innocent woman such as you, especially one as beautiful as you. I am the envy of all of Paris and I intend to have it stay that way. I no longer have any interest in spending all of my time at 'Les Bois Verde in Paris.' I have purchased a small castle in the French-Italian Alps and there, my lovely, you will spend your time as the lady of the manor. I will visit you often, and you shall enjoy spending your time, relaxing, enjoying the Italian sun and, of course, eagerly waiting for my return. There you will find no temptations or allures for illicit affairs, as in this corruptive Paris, and you will remain more pure than the fallen snow and mine, all mine forever."

Upon hearing such news she was angry. She had just gotten accustomed to Paris life and enjoyed the excitement and the attention from all of the men at court. After all, she was not a nun that had to be shut away from human contact. The lady of the manor was just a slave. That's what he wanted her to be! Unfortunately, she had no power, no one to help her and, a week later, they departed for Italy.

The Count left her often and for long periods at a time. She was not allowed to mingle with the town's people but only with her cook, her laundress, private maid and the aged butler for company. She was a lonely woman. Although most pious and dedicated in her religion, she was not allowed to attend services in the main village church, which was back to back with The Castel.

The aged Monsignor came to her private chapel in The Castel to say mass with her and visited her almost every day for prayers and confession. He was the only outsider she spoke to. Unfortunately, he never seemed to have anything to say to her. She always offered him a drink, his being a lover of good food and spirits. He most enjoyed that part of the visit when he was served some of The Castel's fine wine. Then he would politely leave.

It was a warm summer's day. The Castel, with its forty inch thick walls, was always comfortably cool in the summer. From her window and terrace, she could see the town's populace walking, hot with perspiration. She often wished she could feel that way, free to go where she wanted. But this was the life she had chosen and now she had to live with it. She went to the window on bare feet, carefully keeping herself behind the translucent curtains that covered the glass panes. Just below her bedroom window was the parish garden, where daily, the Monsignor and the two priests in residence would walk, pray and meditate.

Here he was as he had been yesterday and every day this week. He must have been new, for she had not seen him before.

He was young, about her age, and if you ignored his black habit, one could see he was very, very hand-some, more like a Roman God than a lowly priest.

With book in hand, he walked along the garden walk deep in prayer. She had timed him a couple of times. He read and prayed for about one hour and then, right under her window on a stone bench facing her, he meditated for another hour. His hour of walking, reading and prayer had just ended. She slowly stepped forward to get a better view. With prayer book in hand, he sat down for rest and meditation, and it was at that exact moment that he looked up, as if praying to God.

The startled look on his face convinced her that it was not God he had seen, but her. Instead of stepping back into the room, she unlocked the window and looking down on him, smiled. The book dropped from his lap. His eyes were transfixed on the vision above him. Even at this distance, she could see his skin take on a reddish blush. In that magic moment their eyes met and both knew that from that moment on, their lives would never be the same again!

The next day she awoke with a headache. Had she not been so lonely and starved for any kind of social contact, she would not have asked for a priest. She knew that the Monsignor would be the one sent to give her confession, for he came every week. She thought it would take at least an hour or two, perhaps longer for the Monsignor to arrive for her daily prayers. He was not due until three o'clock. There was no need for haste.

She did not hear the soft knock on the door until her maid softly called, "Madam, your bath is ready!" The spell was broken. She turned and faced the intruder. "Thank you, Luisa, I'm ready" and walked toward the bath water. The weather was unseasonably warm and humid for May. She didn't like strangers when taking a bath, so she dismissed the maid after the woman had filled the tub.

She undressed herself, hanging her gown on a hanger in the wardrobe. Feeling delightfully wicked, she walked around the room naked, arranging things, until the water in the tin tub cooled enough. She had even examined herself shamelessly in the mirrored doors of the wardrobe. She was nineteen and her breasts weren't very large, but neither were they pendulous. There was no sag at the belly, no flabby flesh hanging from any other part of her perfect body. If anything, she could use a few pounds. She entered the bathtub, washed carefully, but did not soak. Soaking sometimes was debilitating, and she wanted all her strength. She had to be brave and strong today, when in confession with the Monsignor. She wanted to tell him about her feelings as a good Christian wife and ask his advice about her cheating, unfaithful husband, who left her for months at a time to enjoy himself with other women in Paris. She needed someone to talk to, someone to guide her, and he was the only person she knew and could trust.

She emerged and dried herself, sprayed herself with one of the numerous perfumes her husband brought back from France, and then slipped into a dressing gown. She went to the head of the bed, pulled the servants cord, and then went to the door to await his arrival.

"Please tell Pierre to take care of the bath water, Luisa, and then, later, when the Monsignor arrives, have Pierre bring me some wine and cheese—that special wine the Monsignor likes so much."

"It will be done, madam" the maid replied. The maid returned with the butler to help with the bath water and with a cooler of champagne. "I thought perhaps Your Excellency would like a little champagne. It's so refreshing on such a warm day."

"How thoughtful of you," Roxanne replied. She picked up a glass while he opened the bottle and held it out to him, while he poured.

"Thank you very much. That will be all. You may both retire for an afternoon nap and I shall let the old Monsignor in." She walked into the sitting room to put on her dress, combed out her hair, and then sat down at the harp and played music. The champagne made her feel really good.

A few minutes later she heard the door close and then open again. She turned, in some annoyance, wondering what the butler wanted now. But it was not the butler. It was him! There he stood in all his glory. The most handsome fantastic man of the cloth she had ever seen. She tried to speak but could not. His presence had silenced her tongue. Her heart beat so fast that she was certain she was going to faint.

"I knocked several times but no one answered; and the Monsignor told me that you were expecting us and, if no one answered, to just quietly try the door and present myself."

"Yes, of course," she heard herself answer. "The servants are napping. But what happened to the Monsignor?"

"Regrettably, he has the fever and Father Antonio is on an emergency call, so I was the only one available for your daily prayer and confession. I hope you don't mind, and that this has not inconvenienced you."

He seemed nervous, uncomfortable, ill at ease, his hands tightly pressing his prayer book to his bosom as if begging for protection. He was dressed in the common long black dress with numerous tiny black buttons down the front, making him look taller and leaner than his six-feet height. His impeccable pearl-white skin against the coal black wavy hair made his sky-blue eyes look bluer than any Mediterranean Sea. His nose was classical and elegant, and his lips looked strong and tender with a slight upward curve, as if innocently hiding a smile. He bowed once more and followed her as a child would follow a mother.

She was of small stature but her overwhelming beauty was one that demanded respect and admiration for all who witnessed it. She moved as a cloud moves in the sky. Her feet hardly seemed to touch the descending steps. The chapel was small, comfortable and intimate. He walked up to the small alter and she slipped into the pew. He began the prayers and she followed, answering at the proper time. Together they prayed, not as two but as one. It was truly magical and both seemed to be aware of it.

At confession time, she could not speak to this holy man as she had originally planned to do with the Monsignor. He was too young, too beautifully handsome, too excitedly disturbing, to be her confidant. He excited her and made chills go up and down her spine, and activated her imagination to the greatest heights. Her problem would keep till the next time she would meet with the old Monsignor. She demurely thanked the young priest and returned to her rooms.

CHAPTER TWENTY-SEVEN

Confessions

The Monsignor took a bad turn; he had been failing visibly during the last week. Gray marks of exhaustion lay on his lips and eyelids. The fine tremor of his head and his hands had grown pronounced and he was suffering from a bout of influenza.

Masses were said for him and the whole village prayed for his return to good health. The burden of serving the town fell on the two priests. So it was that Father Claudio took over the task of the daily visits to the contessa of The Castel. She was very important to the church as their major weekly contributor.

Claudio was neither afraid nor ignorant of women. Today he had looked with enjoyment upon this young contessa, and seen her exactly as she was—a delightful creature, gifted with feminine graces of voice and body who could make a normal man very happy. He remembered he was a priest and no longer a normal man. He was happy for the world that such women existed and happier yet, that their existence did not seriously disturb his greater love of God.

Daily, he explored the full possibilities of priestly life. He attended the sick, counseled the discouraged and gave solace to those who came to him with human cares. He visited the Countess, as the Monsignor had instructed him. For relaxation he would walk both along the Parish Prayer Garden and around the village. His contact with the outside world was scant. He rarely left The Castel Du Mont and seldom heard from his mother and one old friend.

Into this obscure Eden, the serpent crawled—a beautiful, sweet serpent. Claudio began hearing the whispers of lifeless days in The Castel Du Mont. This was the real threat here. He tried to buoy the knowledge of God's secret ways with his chosen ones. He tried to avoid the woman's eyes; but, seeing her each day was not easy. He hoped that God would loosen his hand a little, to understanding his feelings as he often did with others. Yet, he secretly looked forward each day to his calls at The Castel and Roxanne's confession and prayer time. Irritably, he wondered how any woman could be so honest and provocative at the same time.

Roxanne's mixture of outgoingness and coquetry, her fearless disarming advances—were these the marks of childlike innocence or feminine design? Claudio had never been able to decide, and he could not decide now.

But, after a few meetings, he was beginning to tangle himself into emotional knots about this woman. He recognized the problem as one of those personal, never-quite-to-be-resolved matters, that every man, priest or not, must solve for himself.

The belated ferment now bubbling in Claudio would doubtless make him a mature person and, therefore, a better priest. Yet right now, he needed a bit of emergency treatment. The treatment of choice was to confess to his colleague freely until the throbbing pressure for this woman was reduced. But he could not share his feelings; he never could. He had to fight this all by himself. It had to be just between him and God.

After a while, they were no longer uncomfortable with each other's company. The barriers had been broken. She was now able to forget her royal position and his matching youthful age and good looks and confide in him. She found it even easier than she would have with the Monsignor. He seemed to understand her.

CHAPTER TWENTY-EIGHT

The Internal Anguish

ather Claudio became her most trusted confessor and advisor. She told him of her great unhappiness and her strong resentment for her husband's unfaithfulness and life style. She felt neglected, because he left her alone for months at a time to pursue his pleasures in Paris. She told him of her youth as a poor girl in the streets of Paris, constantly fighting starvation and the reason she had foolishly married the Count, for his class in society, the title of Countess and for security and money.

Nothing else had mattered to her at that time. Now, she knew better! He listened and, as the true pious man he was, he advised her to make the best of it for she had no other choice. Together they prayed for her unhappy life and her salvation. God would help her, he promised.

He had not just become her confessor and her advisor but a good friend as well, and she was most happy for this. He began telling her about his life and his middle-class parents. He had studied for years, and at the age of sixteen he had fallen in love with a most beautiful girl, but she was only fifteen and her parents would not allow him to see her. So the two young lovers met in secret. So much in love were they that during these clandestine meetings, they kissed and made love every minute they were together. "I know I should not be talking to you about such things, but I have never shared this secret with anyone before and, now, I consider you such a good friend, it might help you to understand that life is not an easy road for anyone."

"Oh! Please do go on. I want to hear it all. It's like reading a book! Please go on, please!"

Hesitantly he continued. It felt good to finally share his story with another human being, besides God. So he continued. He told her about how they met for about a year, and one day, she came to him with the wonderful news that she was pregnant with his child. She was so happy and he was so scared. He had another year of schooling before he could get a job as a teacher, but now they had to get married. They had to ask her father's permission. She said not to say anything to anyone; she would speak to her father and mother and meet him on the morrow. That night he could not sleep, he wanted to go to her, talk to her parents and explain how much they were love. But he waited as he had promised her.

The next morning at dawn, when the first town's people went to the well to fetch their fresh drinking water, they found the young girl's body floating in it. Her family was puzzled. They knew she had wanted to get married but had not asked her to whom. They told her that if this was truly love, then love would wait another year.

He did not attend the funeral, nor could he bear to live in that town without her, so he decided to dedicate the rest of his life to God to atone for his sin. He had not spoken to another woman this way in four years.

Roxanne cried, for it was such a sad story. She never felt so close to any other human being before. It was getting to the end of their prayer time, and he led her in one more prayer before he left.

In his room Claudio sought an interior refuge of contemplation in vain. Ever since that afternoon, when he had been ordered to call on the contessa, the corridors of his inner life had been crowded with images of Roxanne. Through scorching afternoons, he was best and not too subtly haunted by fantasies of this woman, with such feminine arms and ivory-pastel flesh. Her economy of movement, which had struck him at first as pleasing, now became painfully retrospect.

The exquisite lift of her eyelashes, the delicate movements of her body as she rose, reached and walked all whirled through his memory. Everything she had ever said to him became an echo, with sheer vibratory excitement. Father Claudio did not dare think of himself as being in love. Yet he could not deny she had touched the central membranes of his heart and mind. Was she reminding him of an earthly happiness that since his priesthood he had denied and no longer dared to dream of?

He now suffered the agonizing consequences of giving one's love disproportionately to anyone but God. It shamed him to realize that Roxanne had gained entrance to the sanctuary reserved for his priesthood and had advanced to the very doors of the tabernacle. She must be turned away before she invaded the sacred precincts where only one love could dwell. Father Claudio, the sworn celibate, the dedicated priest, resolved to turn her away.

CHAPTER TWENTY-NINE

The Beginning of the End

He had made up his mind. After a full night of prayer, he was ready to treat her as just another parishioner with only priestly love in his heart. He strongly believed in the strength of his prayer and his God.

Yet he looked forward each day to his calls on the contessa. Today was a special day; it was her birthday. It had been six months since she had seen her husband, but for her birthday, he had sent her a beautiful diamond necklace. She had decided to wear it. At least Father Claudio would see it; she had to show it to someone besides the servants.

The cook had baked a special cake for her and the butler had made certain to set out the chilled bottle of champagne she loved so much. So per her usual habit, she had dismissed the servants so they could enjoy their daily siesta. She sat on the settee awaiting Father Claudio's visit. She heard the light, timid knock at the door.

"Come in, Father Claudio. How are you today?" She was happy he could see that, in fact, she was radiant.

"Fine Contessa. You look particularly happy for such a dreary, rainy day."

"Look, the cook baked me a cake and the butler insisted on bringing a chilled bottle of champagne. Will you share my birthday with me? You must join me, for a brief repast; you cannot refuse me, especially because it's my birthday!"

The invitation was guileless as a snowflake, but he held off his acceptance.

He remembered that during parish calls, they were not to accept any offerings of drinks or food. First, because it would be a drain on the parishioner's pantry, which, of course, was not the case here. And in the second place, the drinking of coffee, tea or otherwise may lead to relaxation of tongue and mind, which doesn't always turn out to a curate's advantage, and keeps him from remaining the faithful shepherd of his flock.

But this was the Contessa; she was different. He had broken down the walls and even spoken to her of his life. And after all, he was strong in his religion. A piece of cake and a sip of champagne could not drown in the sea of the greater love that buoyed him as he floated on its sustaining wave.

It would be very innocent, but Claudio knew that

some pleasures, innocent though they might be, were not for him. The priesthood required an extraordinary self-discipline and perfect trust. "When my test comes," prayed Claudio, "grant, Lord, that I shall not murmur against the rigors of the love." His most difficult task was now at hand.

He was a bit taken back at her flippant attitude toward him today. But it was her birthday, and she looked so beautiful and happy, he could not refuse her. "On one condition that, as soon as we finish this little repast, we go to the chapel and pray."

"I promise" she muttered demurely. "Please pour the champagne and I will cut the cake. It's my favorite. It is saturated with rum that usually makes me feel so good. You will love it too, I promise." He smiled. She certainly was in a wonderful mood.

The cake was most delectable and the champagne, with its tiny bubbles that tickled your nose, gave one an exhilarating feeling, making them both feel so warm and tingling, like two free does in the woods.

"Please, another glass, please," she asked. "It makes me so warm and happy." He refilled the heavy, deep cut crystal glasses. This magic, bubbly drink indeed made one happy. As he handed her the glass, their fingers touched. As if lightning struck them, they felt that electrifying force from one body to the other, as if feeding them eternal strength and binding them forever.

Looking at each other over the crystal glasses of champagne, they gulped the mystic drink, releasing all fears and inhibitions. In his eyes, she was now a young maiden and he just a young normal man, and both were very much in love. As the greatest tidal wave of a typhoon hit the century-old rocks, his strength, hit by such force, broke off his guard into tiny pieces and came down upon him crushing him. The great fire that had been burning within him for so long exploded, leaving him no longer the dedicated man of God, but a mere human being, as the tide slowly swept away all of his godly dedications.

Without a word, his dark head lowered as he drew her closely to him. Roxanne felt the heated drumming of her heart, the surge of her pulse, and then he kissed her. His mouth was as warm and firm as she had felt in her dreams. She should have twisted away. He gently put up a hand to cradle the back of her head, his fingers tunneling into the heavy mane of her hair, while his other arm curved around her back, to pull her even more closely against him. Claudio's mind was beyond any rational thinking. He did not recognize himself but felt as if he were watching someone else.

Roxanne moaned, wondering why she was allowing him such liberties. She knew she could have stopped rain from falling more easily than she could have stopped Father Claudio from kissing her.

Although shy, he was also a determined man, with the determination of a man that had fought against this great love, this great desire to have her, for a very long time. Oh! How he had fought his feelings and desires. He had prayed to God to help him get over the infatuation for this woman. He had asked the other priest to take over the task of the daily visitations at The Castel, but this had been refused.

With the monsignor ill, it was Father Antonio who was now the curate and in charge. He had the rest of the village people to take care of. So Father Claudio had to continue with The Castel visits and endure the guilt and torture of his unrequited love. He prayed, prayed constantly for God to help, but where was God now? Had all his prayers been in vain?

His life had been pure torment ever since he had first met her. She had been in his dreams, awake and sleeping. Nothing meant anything to him anymore but wanting to be with her. He was her prisoner, prisoner of love, and now he was lost.

Roxanne wondered how she could be hot and cold at the same time? Shivering, and yet flushed with heat, she knew she loved the feel of his mouth. His mouth drifted in a searching path up the line of her jaw to her ear, then down the smooth column of her throat. Her eyes closed; his heavy brows and thick-lashed eyes seemed to see right past her pathetic resistance to the longing beneath. What were they doing? When his hands moved to cup her hips and pull her body up hard against him, Roxanne felt the rigid thrust of his male body against her stomach, so different from her husband's aging, softer-toned body.

It shocked her and frightened her. She could not clearly think what was happening, but she loved it. And now, there seemed to be a drastic change. His lips were more insistent, his hands more daring, and there was the nudging prod of him against her in a way that was arousing. His mouth covered hers again and she instinctively arched into him instead of away. Her body reacting with shock, the movements brought her formally against him and she could feel the unyielding length of his body against her, nudging urgently into the soft round of her stomach. His tongue slid between her lips in deep thrusts as he ground his lips against hers. She was bewildered by the curling fire deep in her stomach, making even her thighs ache for him. It wasn't right; it wasn't normal; there had to be something inherently wrong with what they were doing or it would not feel so deliciously wicked.

He explored her open mouth with hot kisses. She felt him shudder, and he gently untied all the laces of her chemise to pull it down around her waist. His hand over her naked breasts made her body feel entirely boneless and her knees buckled.

"What's happening?" she sobbed. He didn't speak for a moment. He couldn't. All his male urges were too hot and high for him to risk saying anything to her until he regained control. Just one glance at Roxanne's classical features and the thick sweep of her hair that gleamed in the candlelight had long made him forget his priesthood. She had ignited a fire in him, a deep coiling fire that raged through him and left all his good intentions in ashes. The reality of what was happening to her, with her abandoned response to his exploring hands, seemed quite different from any vague imaginings of the past experiences with her husband. Softly murmuring his name, she felt him shivering against her as she felt him curl his fingers in the material of her dress and slide it from her body. She now boldly worked her nimble fingers at the buttons of his pants and released that part of him that was so urgently pressing her, and circling it with her fingers. She felt his leaping response and a sense of excitement for being able to prompt such a shivering reaction from him. And then, he did the same to her. He picked her up and carried her to the bed. His hands moved to stroke between her thighs, with lingering motions that made her writhe. Roxanne could not stop her cries.

Her soft cries only spurred Claudio to greater effort, and when she convulsed, he smothered the cries with his mouth. Slowly, his tongue traced hot, searing patterns over her body, making her cry out. She could feel the heat of him against her, prodding insistently into her, and then with a sudden thrust of his body, a slight pain knifed through her. He was so large and he held her fast as she tried to wiggle away, his hands hard on her waist to keep her still. He held her, still not moving, but waited until she stopped shaking. He began to lift her, rocking her on top of him in gentle thrusts as the pain of his penetration lessened.

She began to match his quickening rhythm. It did not hurt her anymore. Instead, she began to feel a return of the earlier tension. The aching need built swiftly into a rising urgency and, when it crescendod into a hot, soaring release, she cried out against him.

CHAPTER THIRTY

The Beginning of the End

He had made up his mind. After a full night of prayer, he was ready to treat her as just another parishioner with only priestly love in his heart. He strongly believed in the strength of his prayer and his God.

Count Du Pons was a well-known aristocrat. His father, "His Highness Count Alexander Du Pons," had died more than twenty years ago, but his title and reputation still carried a great deal of power in international society. The present Count Du Pons' maternal grandfather had also been a member of the Roman Black Society. He was the son of Thomas Bragiotti, who had inherited membership into the society.

These Blacks or "Neri" were great supporters of the Royal House of Savoy and took part in several of the Italian affairs. But the society's membership—rich men with very little to do—had escaped into a make-believe

world of manners. They had lifted etiquette to the condition of an art, as outmoded, perhaps, as falconry, but an
art, nevertheless, which the Count proudly introduced
to Parisian society.

The system had elaborate rules. In certain houses,
some of the older men wore a glove only on the left
hand, leaving the right hand bare. In other houses both
hands were gloved, but the thumb of the right hand
was exposed. Two theories lay behind this practice.
The glove was originally a sign of nobility; you never
see a peasant with a glove on. The glove traditionally
was always associated with the sword. The right hand,
some felt, had to be left encumbered, the better to draw
the sword in defense of your sovereign. Also, one hand
had to be ungloved in order to accept the hand of a host
the moment it was offered. Any delay would have been
construed as unfriendly.

Those exposed-thumb families, who had such
high and important ancestors, could not be expected
to give their entire hand to late comers. These were
lucky to get a thumb and forefinger. Only a few of
the purists remained, but the Count Armando Du
Pons, deeply rooted in his "Orgolio," for self-esteem,
was among them. Gloves had always been a part of
his costumes.

He was an outstanding dresser, with his blown
hair and moustache, his jaunty stride, flushed face and

unbuttoned fur coat. With his hat at a rakish angle, he always seemed so unconcerned, as though he were going to a party. This was the present casual look of Parisian Society.

Many hundreds of miles from The Castel Du Mont, away from his beloved, beautiful, sheltered wife, the Count was completely emerged in Parisian social life. He loved his gorgeous, young pure wife, but after so many years of practicing the numerous sexual acts of his liking, he was forced to pursue this type of life away from her in Paris.

He had just ordered his cabriolet and told the driver to take him to 36 Vie De La Perue. As he exited his flat, there was his coach parked by the curb. It was a dreary, typical autumn, lightly rainy Paris day, so dreary he had to do something to cheer up.

As he arrived at his destination, there was already another coach parked in front. He walked up the stone steps and twisted the doorbell. It was answered in a moment by the butler. "Please present my card to Mrs. Bernet," he said "and inform her that I would be most grateful for the courtesy of being received."

The butler looked at the card and, completely un-abashedly, read it and allowed his eyebrows to rise. "Count Du Pons, please do come in." The Count was very much aware of the fact that his name and person-al card could get him into any place in London and

Paris. After all, the Du Pons were a very old Aristocratic French family; they had fought the Romans and the Germans and had been victorious each time.

A tall, handsome, red-haired woman of about thirty years old, who hardly looked twenty and dressed in the latest French fashion, entered the sitting room. She tapped the card in her hand. "Count Du Pons is it?" she asked in a voice he thought sounded like a bell.

"Yes" he answered with a bow. He had the odd notion that she expected her hand to be kissed. Instead, making what he recognized to be an awkward little bow, he took her hand and shook it gently. That seemed to arouse her anger.

"I'm afraid I don't quite understand," she said. The Count was both infuriated and unnerved by her awareness, and that he was regarded as just another person. His face colored; he was furious. No one had ever treated him in such a manner. Who did this whore, this trollop, think she was when she was just the daughter of a mere merchant? It was a fact that she had spent more time in French beds with just about every noble male of Paris.

She, knowing exactly the reaction she aroused in him, smiled that certain smile of one who had just received the triumph card. "I am having tea; perhaps you will be good enough to follow me."

He had to restrain himself from storming away, but

he had long ago learned that whenever he had lost his temper, he lost the battle. He nodded, not trusting himself to speak, and followed her into the garden room.

"By chance, do you gentlemen know each other?"

"Indeed we do," answered Duke Le Blanc. "Count Du Pons is one of our more distinguished citizens and a man of excellent taste. How good to see you. Sorry that I must leave you; another appointment, you see." With that, he turned around and walked out.

It was rather an awkward moment followed by a pause of silence. The Count had a shaming thought "What am I doing here? What do I want? He had heard of the high praises of Madam Bernet's Charms, and he thought he might savor some. But it was not turning out as he had planned, and she was sitting across from him on the settee, smug before the fireplace as if she wanted him to beg her.

Well, he would fix her wagon. He'd just stand up and walk out. She stood up and, as she swept past him, he got a nose full of her scent. It was absolutely wicked. He followed her to a grand bedroom with a four poster bed and a large mirror above. He remembered his friend Monsieur Carott saying, "She will give you a good time; anything you want if you know what I mean."

He met the eyes of the woman who looked at him with an excited expression. "Would you like me to take off my clothes, or would you prefer doing it yourself?

You may do whatever your heart desires. I am all yours to love, to play, to enjoy."

He was thankful he had not walked out, for the foreplay that followed was worth going to Hell for. She was truly a fantastic woman!

CHAPTER THIRTY-ONE

Tragic Return

The cold hard truth was that she had missed her time of the month, and it was the very first time it had ever happened since she had been fourteen years old. The other girls in the catholic school sometimes had missed their period. There was a possibility that she had missed it solely because of the excitement. Maybe sex had stopped it; maybe not. Then what? She had prayed to God that she wouldn't be pregnant, but that seemed rather futile if God wanted her to be pregnant. She would have three more weeks before she could be certain. She wanted her lover's child so much—their love child. She had no one to confide with, no one from whom to seek advice. She crept along the hall and her nightgown brushed against her calves and ankles. The last image from the full moon cast sharp moon beams through the window. The rest of the place was in complete darkness. She listened for sounds of anyone stirring. All was quiet, while, through the door, she could hear a bell tolling midnight somewhere.

The sound of footsteps awakened her. She had no idea how long she had been asleep, no idea what time it might be. She sat up, startled, and then felt panic grip her. She recognized the footsteps.

He had a long lazy stride; and those tall black knee boots he wore made a certain ring along the marble floor. She jumped to her feet, her heart was pounding. What was she afraid of? It sounded like her husband, but he was in Paris on business! It could not be him, she told herself. She could not bear being touched by him now that she had finally experienced true love.

Moonlight spilled through the windows, and the room was filled with hazy silver light, every detail clear. The footsteps stopped outside the bedroom door. Had she locked it? No, of course she hadn't.

Oh! It was him all right. She knew he wanted something— that something he was entitled to as a husband; but it was something she was not prepared to give anymore. She had always been so passive about his lovemaking, never truly feeling part of it and always as if just watching someone else. But now it was different. Paralyzed with fear, she stared at the door and saw the doorknob slowly turning. Then, the door opened and he stepped inside. Count Du Pons, for a second, lounged in the doorway one shoulder propped against the jamb, almost as if wondering. As if he shouldn't wake her. He feigned sleep.

He gazed at her with those dark mocking eyes and his full sensual lips, still toying with a smile, at the beautiful maiden he had made his wife. He had taken her to this deserted castle to keep her pure, away from the corrupt Parisian courts and low morality of the city life. He had been determined never to share this beauty with anyone. She was his and his alone.

He would return to Paris every now and then to indulge himself in city talk, and to enjoy other maidens, but he always made certain that this one would be waiting for him—pure and forever. Now at the age of fifty-one, he wore his magnetism with casual disdain, as all rich men do. Taking it for granted with any woman they encountered, they knew the women would succumb at the snap of their finger. Most of the women did, and he accepted their adulation somewhat wearily, considering it no more than his due.

He noted a slight flutter of her eyelids. "I see you are awake angel" he remarked as he slowly lifted the candle by the bedside. "You seem a bit upset. Did I startle you in barging in at such an ungodly hour? I have just arrived and could not wait to see your lovely face once more. You are most beautiful when half asleep." He slowly kissed her on her cheek.

She looked at him, striving to maintain some kind

of composure, fighting to conceal her alarm. He was her husband and she had never felt such a feeling of repulsion before. He noted this apprehension and, for some unknown explanation, he almost enjoyed it. He was so utterly relaxed for a man who had traveled for almost four days by carriage to reach her. He slowly undressed, removing his gloves and traveling garments carefully and deliberately.

He smiled as he sauntered across the room towards her, stopping directly in front of her. He was so close she could smell the male musk odor of flesh and perspiration. "We are going to make good love tonight, my dear. It has been a long time." His smile flashed and his eyes filled with dark amusement. His face was inches away from hers, and she could see that familiar scar at the corner of that full curving mouth. (He had received that scar in a duel.) She noted the smudges under his eyes, a result of the long voyage. Her heart was beating rapidly, and she was trembling inside. She wanted her lover, her true love. Where was he now; where was Claudio?

She detested this old man. She was afraid of him, and his nearness caused her great panic.

"No, please," she whispered. He stared at her with disbelief. A lock of dark, graying hair fell across his brow. He reached up to push it back.

"You are beautiful, my darling wife, the most

beautiful woman on earth. You're my young wife, and I have been away from you too long. I'm going to make you happy. You've no idea of the new things I've experienced in Paris."

Slowly with lazy deliberation, he pulled her into his arms. As she tried to pull away, he laughed slowly to himself, tightening his grip. His eyes gleamed, holding hers, and his wide lips parted as he tilted his head, pulling her close. She opened her mouth to protest but before she could speak, his mouth fastened over hers. It was a long practiced kiss, his lips pressing and probing, savoring her lips.

In his passion he did not notice she was rigid in his arms as he continued to kiss her. Then weakness came, and she melted against him against her will. When he finally released her, for he wasn't ready yet, his eyes were dark with triumph.

"Now that you are a grown woman, you need a man more often my darling. A woman like you will always need a man. That's the way you're made, and I'll try to spend much more time with you. You're finally ripe to be fully plucked, and you're hungry for more of it."

She tried to speak but her throat was dry. He stood up and pulled back the covers and, with those dark eyes, he was taking in every detail as if seeing her beauty for the very first time. Her hair cascaded about her shoulders. Her low petticoat nightgown, with its clinging bodice, left her shoulders and most of her bosom bare. "Your hair, your body—it's a crime to hide a body like this. I've known a lot of women, but never any so utterly superb. I'm going to touch you all over and you are going to love it."

Panic overwhelmed her, and she began to struggle as he laughed huskily. Young maidens were always so skittish about lovemaking. He wrapped his arms around her, one arm tightly around her waist, as he lifted her hair and planted his lips against the side of her neck and slowly slid his tongue in her ear. Her flesh seemed to burn. He cupped one large hand around her breast. He was in no hurry, no hurry at all.

Tears spilled down her cheeks as she shook her head away. When she refused to look his way, his fingers groped tightly, hurting her. He seized her hair with his left hand and tugged, forcing her head to tilt back to look at his face, now stamped strongly with desire.

Then he kissed her hard and unyielding, as he would kiss a whore, forcing her lips to open so that his tongue could plunge and probe the same way his fingers were probing below. She trembled all over.

"Not like this, please" she begged, "It should not happen this way, in anger without tenderness. Please don't. You might hurt the baby!"

Caught up in the frenzy of his lust, not listening to what she was saying, he made a deep growling noise, and then he whipped up her petticoat jerked down the top of his underwear, and fell upon her. She was an object, a receptacle for his lust. She had tried to throw him off. She fought him and fought herself. She fought the sensation exploding inside her, though he thrust inside her brutally as inflicting a harsh punishment. Then, there was nothing but need and he cried out her name and held her tightly.

She was crying softly. With a deadly anger he shouted, "Baby? What baby? Who is he . . . this man that made you pregnant?" And he shook her so hard that she fainted.

She did not know how long she had been unconscious. She only knew that she had been extremely beaten, her body ached as it never had ached before. Her face felt painful and swollen. Her ears rang with the cries of her husband. "Cheat on me, will you? I always knew you were a slut, and now you proved it. Don't tell me it is mine; I'm not that gullible. Speak who is it?" And, when she just whispered "yours," he beat her again, now and through the whole long night. But Roxanne was determined never to reveal the name of her lover, even if it killed her.

Now that he was back, things seemed different. She stared glumly at the marble floors and the ceilings with their painted frescoes. At first the rooms in The Castel had been snug and wonderful. She had loved playing the Lady of The Castel, so different from the ugly streets of Paris, where she had lived in extreme poverty until the Count had found her. But since having fallen in love with Claudio, she found these rooms confining. And now with her husband's return, she felt like a prisoner with him watching her every move. She endured nights of angry frustration, submission to her wifely duties, and a loneliness that grew stronger and more tormenting as the weeks passed.

CHAPTER THIRTY-TWO

Return to Paris

The Monsignor rose from his sick bed to say Mass at The Castel now that the Count was in residence. Unbeknown to the Count and Roxanne, Father Claudio had left the parish for places unknown, and another older priest had taken his place.

The Count could not obtain any information of any lover from any of the dedicated servants or anyone else in town. So he tried to convince himself that maybe, just maybe this could possibly be his child. After all, he still considered himself a virile man.

And so a week later, in a disappointed fugitive fashion, he closed The Castel Du Mont, dismissing all of the servants but the caretaker. He never wanted to come back here again, and in his formal black carriage, with his pregnant wife, sped away toward Paris, the city of gaiety and sin. The driver of the carriage, ominously large and cloaked in black, pulled on the reins and hurled an oath down at the team of dapple grays, but his voice was lost beneath the heavy thud of hounding hooves and a rattle of churning wheels. The noise of the ride echoed in the chilling night until it seemed to come from every direction.

Night whipped the villages with cold, misty darkness. The threat of winter was heavy in the air. Acrid smoke stung the nostrils and throat, for in every home, fires were stirred and stoked against the chill that pierced the bones. Low-hanging clouds dribbled fine droplets of moisture which mixed with the soot spewed forth from the towering chimneys before falling as a thin film that covered every surface.

The miserable night masked the passage of a carriage that careened through the narrow streets, as if it was fleeing to some terrible disaster. It jolted and tottered precariously over the cobblestones of the villages, its high wheels sending mud and water splattering. In the calm that followed the coach's passing, the murky liquid trickled slowly back to mirrored pools packed with droplets of neatly patterned ripples.

Roxanne was little concerned with the muck beyond the leather shades or, indeed, with anything but her own thoughts. She sat in silence, her face devoid of expression. Now and then, the lantern would swing into a jolting lurch of the carriage and its weak light would catch the hard brittle gleam in the depths of her eyes. No man gazing into them would have found a trace of warmth to cheer him on or any hint of love to comfort his heart.

"Claudio, where are you? Will I ever see you again?" her heart cried, letting her mind probe once again as if trying to find a solution to her dilemma. She looked at her husband, seated facing her, his angry glare burning into her. This was one of those times which demanded all of her cunning, and she was desperate enough to try anything.

Roxanne, drawing aside the leather shades at the window, peered out into the night. Shreds of fog had begun to seep into the streets, half masking the darkened homes as they passed them. It was a most dark, dreary night, but she could abide fog and dampness. It was storms she feared, lending little comfort and peace to her mind and heart when they raged across the land.

Letting the shade fall into place again, Roxanne closed her eyes, finding no release for her tension. In an effort to still the trembling that possessed her, she pressed her slender hands deep into her muff, stretching them tightly together over her abdomen as if trying to protect that living being within her, her most precious possession. Somewhere a bell tolled in the night. Time hung motionless as uncertainty pecked at the outer limits of her mind. Why had things turned out so badly? Who was this God that allowed her to find the one she truly loved and then grasped everything away? What kind of God was this? But no voices gave the answers Roxanne sought. There was only the steady drumming of the horse's hooves, bringing them ever closer to their destination.

They had been traveling three days and had rested three nights at roadside inns. She felt journey-worn, almost completely physically and mentally exhausted and so fearful that anymore time spent in this jostling carriage might cause her to lose her baby. The carriage eased its relentless pace and swung around the corner as it rumbled to a stop in the circular driveway before the forbidding facade of "Les Bois Verde," her husband's ancestral estate.

How well she remembered her early days in this place. How much she had loved Countess Du Pons, and how she had loved living here! All now was gone. How kind her husband was then, how caring. In the meager light cast by the carriage lantern, his eyes met hers and his brow wore an angry frown. "You better make yourself ready my wife, as we have arrived."

She set her mind with cool deliberation, pulling a heavy laced veil down over her face, trying to hide from the servants the marks he had inflicted upon her face three nights before, and adjusted the deep hood of her black velvet cloak. He led the way toward the main portal, where the footman was already waiting for them. Roxanne fought an urge to flee in the opposite direction, but checked the impulse, reasoning that this was madness. There was nothing she could do. Without money and no place to which she could go, she silently followed the man she loathed. "Here, madam is where you will live and give birth to the baby you claim to be mine." She was set to shriek her fury in his face, but his laughing rang in the high ceiling anteroom and brought a quick death to her ire. Her jaw dropped and the urge to kill him was strong.

She had no recourse but to bear his senseless tormenting. She could only bestow upon him a glare of such hate that it should have set the very blood in his veins boiling. But the proud man bore the pain of an unfaithful wife with some dignity and, in front of the servants, struggled to control his mirth.

"Come, you must be tired, madam. Let us retire."

She undressed hurriedly as he gave commands to the servants and hurried into the bed before he could even get a glimpse of her. She sat there observing him with fear in her eyes. Turning to her, he came with that sure stride and, even in her predicament, he seemed not to care.

Outside, the dark clouds gathered, deepening the blackness of the night. She paused to listen to the sound of the wind, blowing about the corners of the house. It rose forlornly and whistled eerily at a higher pitch. Raindrops splattered against the windows and ran down them in streams. His deep voice seemed to reverberate within her very sole as he announced, "And now, my dear wife, to your wifely duty." Rattling gusts of rain struck the building and the wind howled like a banshee in the gathering gloom of the dying night.

It was his smug conceit, self-satisfying, and overwhelming sneering expression she hated most. Roxanne cried with deep frustration. She wished she were dead.

"This is where the trollops like you belong and will spend the rest of your miserable life watching me cheat on you with many different women. I haven't fought that it is my child. And, if it truly is, then lady, you just picked the wrong time to get pregnant, without asking me first."

No matter what he said or how he treated her, she did not care. Her only purpose in life now was the child she was carrying in her womb, his child, Claudio's child!

He slowly came to bed and, suddenly, she realized his hand was already beneath her nightgown and boldly high on her thigh. She grasped his wrist and tugged it away only to find that on her shoulders his fingers were lowering the ribboned straps of her gown.

His fingers were feeling her bosom. "Nay, madam, yield to me now, my love!" he murmured thickly, against her throat. His face lowered, his mouth was scalding upon her breast and he was devoured in a searing scorching flame that shot through him like a flaming rocket. Suddenly, it seemed he had twice the normal number of hands. Her own flew in a flurry for protection. She caught both of his and hugged them tight against her midriff in an effort to keep them still. Then a new realization dawned. In the struggle, her gown had been pulled from beneath her and her bare buttocks rested full against his loins. His manhood beneath the silken sheets was bold and hard against her. Even now, his hands were slipping away from her grasp and creeping up her side, pulling her closer to him.

"Sir, you are no gentleman," she gasped in outrage.

"Did you expect me to be after all that's happened?"

"You are a cad," she panted, trying to pry his hands away.

The Count laughed softly and his breath brushed her throat. "Only a husband," he replied, "well warmed and willing."

She wanted to cry out, but who would come to her side. She struggled with renewed energy. Then his hand was hot upon her naked breast, and her free hand snapped forward like a striking falcon. But it was stopped a bare inch from his laughing face. With much urgency, his teeth showing in a savage snarl, he cursed her viciously. His grip was iron hard and gave her great pain. He clasped both her wrists behind the small of her back.

Roxanne drew a breath to shriek in anger, but his mouth smothered her outcries. Her head rolled in an ever quickening reaction and she struggled against the intoxication of his obnoxious kiss.

"Sir," she gasped as his lips lifted from hers, "Don't, please don't."

He moved and was hot and hard between her thighs. Her lips were dry and, in a last weak effort, tried to shield herself from his probing staff.

"I'm a man of flesh and blood and your husband as well. I'm no monster, lady," he rasped, and urgently and with much force came to her. At first a sharp piercing pain made her gasp, followed by a warmth deep inside that made her sob, fearing that it might injure the baby.

"God, please help me! Please help me!" she cried.

"Ohhhh, damn," the Count groaned in frustrated agony. "Damn you, deceiving little bitch!" He snatched her roughly and flung her away.

In the dim light, his sneering eyes raked her cruelly, with her pale quivering breasts and the soft lovely thighs still naked to his gaze. "Cover yourself," he groaned out derisively. "I am through with you for now." A ragged growl tore from his throat and, before she could speak, he dashed back to his private bedroom and left Roxanne wondering if this is what her life was doomed to be.

The Count often thought of killing this woman whose magnificent body grew, swollen with a human being, but finally his pride and machismo convinced him that this was his child. After all, he was very young for his age and most sexually active. It had to be his child. It was!

The Castel Du Mont was kept closed for many years. It remained an inanimate, desolate place.

BOOK FOUR

CHAPTER THIRTY-THREE

Penitence

With his whole world falling down around him, Father Claudio could not remember walking back to his room. His mind was in a complete veil of denial. The past events must have happened to someone else, not to him, whose greatest devotion had been only to God.

He looked at the time and realized he had to rush to conduct the evening mass. Like a zombie, with movements as automatic as that of the pendulum in a clock, he walked into the House of God.

It was nearing the end of the mass, and twilight was wrapping the sacristy in violet gauze when he carried the sacred goblet back to the cabinet. This final service completed, he stood at the bottom of the stairs to the altar as he finished the mass. "I now leave the altar of God as a tarnished sinner," he thought. The sun was beginning to descend when Father Claudio stole out of the church.

He had not heard Father Antonio asking him if anything had happened, or why he was so pale. He just looked up at him not knowing or being able to say anything.

"Feel like walking? It will do us both good," said Father Antonio. A long intimate walk would give Claudio a chance to blow off some emotional steam. Claudio's "no" answer just encouraged Father Antonio to continue. Something had to be very wrong if Father Claudio, the master of alibis could not answer. They began walking. Claudio, at the bottom of his adolescent soul, was framing the overwhelming confession he wanted so desperately to be in conversation. A street lamp, obscured by an elm trunk, threw a corona of light on Father Claudio's tormented face. Father Claudio stood still, surprised by his own confession. Tears, blue under the street lamp, streamed down his cheeks. The hurt was twisting his nervous system. Right now he needed a bit of emergency treatment and advice.

Father Antonio decided to let Father Claudio talk freely. The night air was an aphrodisiac of turf and summer. They leaned over the railing of the drawbridge and gazed down at the black water of the moat. A marshy smell, oldest of the aphrodisiacs, rose from the blackish water as it sailed past the membranes of their nostrils with associations more ancient than man.

Father Claudio quietly murmured, "Women have

the power of reminding ordinary men that love exists. That is as God intended it to be. But as a priest, we should be moved by another power, not the physical accidents of love, but love itself."

They were walking again in silence.

"Father Antonio," he blurted out with great flow of agitation, guilt and passion, "Today I sinned with a woman!" Father Antonio, for a moment taken completely off guard, was silent. Never before had he heard such a declaration from a priest. How could one help or try to comfort someone so tortured!

Father Antonio responded, "Father, as you well know, there is no way a simple priest as I could properly advise you. This advice must come from a higher authority. It should be better solved between you and God himself." They walked the rest of the way in complete silence, desperation and prayer. Alone in his room, Father Claudio stripped off his outer clothing and sat by the open window of his room, trying to cool off. But, now the mixed tensions of the day began to take their delayed claim. The spiritual tourniquet, tightly applied was slowly released. Mortal tide flowed back into his limbs and organs, bringing unbearable pain.

The contessa's wonderful body and seductive voice, the desperate "oh!" and the memory of uncontrollable lovemaking, the dreadful sin he had committed against his God—all of these things began to bring images before him and churn in his bloodstream. He knew well that his mortal sin would never be forgiven or forgotten. He gazed out of the window and felt the non-perfumed flowers of duty and obligation. Over the mountain range climbed the pale profile of a new moon, climbing from another part of the earth. Soon there would be another day; but would there ever be another day for him?

He had prayed and prayed all night for some advice, some word from The One he had offended. A few times he lay down to sleep, but sleep would not come. Would he ever be able to sleep again? He closed his eyes and wept and wept impotent tears of grief and shame.

He felt a tremendous weight of the sin he had committed. He was assailed by the very temptation to believe that he had been forsaken by God, that his priesthood had been in vain, and that the weight of mortal grief and sin had been more than he could bear in the midst of this anguish. He asked of Him, a sign, some visible way of his unchanging light, in a world of hideous darkness.

He was very sorry that this visible sign had not been given. The burning bush of Moses, the jewel and crusted dove of Theresa, The Tolle Lege of Augustine—these, he realized, were no longer the style as in the simpler days of saints and prophets. The light he hoped would be interior, he must look for within. But no light came; there was no light and he was disconsolate.

He slipped his hand into the pocket of his black coat, and pulled out his breviary and read without serenity and much devotion, for only in prayer could he hope for some type of tranquility. That night while he was kneeling in his bedroom, his plea lifted to God, The Almighty Himself, to Him who cannot refuse pardoning anything or anyone. He asked in the name of forgiveness and love. He stormed Heaven with Litany of The Blessed Virgin. But he knew, even if the ever-forgiving God could forgive him, he could never forgive himself.

Before dawn, he had packed a few clothes, written a note of goodbye and before even Father Antonio had risen for the six o'clock mass, Father Claudio slipped out of the church, out of the village, to the monastery way up in The Alps. Only an unwillingness to lead himself out to morbid scourging saved Father Claudio from the emotional luxury of throwing himself in the dark, fast-running river. He sat by the water face down with hands shielding his eyes and confessed to God once more the nature's ode, his desire, and again he prayed and prayed for forgiveness.

Dust of an eight-mile walk from the nearest village lay on Father Claudio's black coat as he tugged at a bell pool dangling from the front door. The monastery on the rim of The Alpine "Campagnia," might have been a powder magazine, a military prison or a pest house for contagious diseases at various times. It had been all of these, with its gloomy cemetery, filled with frightful examples of baroque statuary, where war heroes' bones lay in sterile dust alongside the victims of cholera, smallpox, and other epidemics no longer in fashion. The building had fallen into shunned neglect until a group of Benedictines had taken it over as a monastery. By skillful and diligent management, the disciples of Saint Benedict had rebuilt the moldering pile, dispersed the unwholesome vapors surrounding it, and given the place a quiet reputation in the field of religion. From all parts of Europe, visitors came to the Benedictine Monastery to make a spiritual retreat under the saintly direction of Dom Domenico Belotti.

Father Claudio was dubious and depressed about making this retreat. Could Dom Belotti help his suffering sinful human soul? He yanked the bell again. A little window opened as the tonsured head of a young man popped out as if from a cuckoo clock. The young man had a soup bowl haircut and a cast in one eye— a combination that made him seem none too bright.

"I've come to make a spiritual retreat," said Father Claudio. There was an inner rattling of bolts. "Dom Belotti's orders are to let the retreatant in and show him courteously to his cell."

The door swung open and Father Claudio saw a

lubberly lay brother who had outgrown his coarse, brown tunic. His red wrists projected from short sleeves, and he was barefoot. A blast of kitchen odors gushed from him as he reached for Father Claudio's bag.

Father Claudio followed the guide down the stone corridor to the iron-hinged door and preceded him into the cell. He surveyed his cell, furnished with standard and anchorite gear and an iron cot, a straw mattress, one blanket and two coat hooks. A kneeling bench and a crucifix at eye level hung slightly askew on a rough plaster wall.

He removed his collar, hung his dusty coat on a hook and gazed out the curtain-less window at the monuments of the cemetery. Unable to pray any longer or meditate, he lay down on the straw mattress and gave himself up to thoughts that he could not drive from his mind. He remembered the famous Italian proverb, "Love makes time pass, time makes love pass."

Tossing on his monastic cot, Father Claudio waited for the wonder-working Dom Belotti to appear. "Sorry for the delay" declared Dom Belotti, "I have listened for the last five hours to all the other problems, and now I am prepared to spend the night listening to yours."

Load-weary, Father Claudio began to unpack his heart. Tentatively at first, and then with increasing confidence, he traced the course of his sinful event. During the recital, Dom Belotti, watched the young man's lips.

Not until he had stopped altogether did he make his first comment.

"Tell me something of your youth, your family and your general background." Father Claudio took a deep breath, then shot down the foaming rapids of memory. He spoke of his parents and siblings, of the young girl he had impregnated, of her death, and of the great admiration he still felt about the mysteries of women.

"I gather you developed a profound sense of guilt about your sexual temptations."

"I did. This guilt increased when I entered the seminary. Dedicated to the priestly life, I found myself torn between an ideal of chastity and yearning for women. The conflict was so great that at one time I was deeply concerned as to whether I should continue my studies for the priesthood. I should have given it up then."

"By what means did you solve this conflict?"

"By the means I always used when going was the hardest. I increased my devotions, prayed for the gift of supernatural grace and held on somehow from day to day—until that faithless day. It was never easy!"

"Father Claudio, this is the case of an offender who carefully selected a sin that should never have materialized—a Lucifer who dares to take the consequences of open revolt against either the earthly or the Heavenly Father. Can you deny the pitiful mechanics of this plot against yourself?"

"I have no desire to deny anything except that this was not premeditation. I strongly fought against it," said Father Claudio.

"I will speak to the Cardinal himself of this matter, and he will advise accordingly." Dom Belotti turned toward the door and walked out.

After a long, agonizing dark night, Claudio came to the conclusion that Roxanne had and always would mean more to him than the Almighty God he had sworn to serve. He was not, as he had hoped, a true man of the cloth, but a mere mortal, with the same feelings and desires as those of his parishioners.

Suicide had entered his mind numerous times in these last couple of days, but it would have been a coward's way out of his miserable existence, and another sin against the Lord. He was well aware that his desire for her would burn in him for the rest of his life; but, as Judas, he would always feel a betrayer to the God he had sworn to serve. To dedicate whatever was left of his tainted being and to apply himself to the most difficult, unbearable sacrifices a human could endure, was his only solution.

Yes, of course, he would request he be transferred to one of the Leper colonies, where pain, physical and mental, would be part of his daily hours and where he could, at least, try to help those suffering beings that, unlike him, in most cases had not been sinners, but for some unknown reason, had been dealt a life of misery and pain.

The next day, after the painful confession with Dom Belotti and with the approval of the Cardinal and the blessing of his ailing Monsignor, he left for his chosen life of Hell.

CHAPTER THIRTY-FOUR

Payment of Sin

He had arrived in Africa, where the air was stifling. Two small, black urchins led him down a lane so narrow that they were forced to walk two abreast, while their shoulders brushed against the high overgrown bushes on either side. He stopped before a wrought iron gate with two African masks scrolled with the name, "Lady of Solace Refuge" above the entry. This was the Leper colony to which Father Claudio had been sent. Corrugated iron sheets behind the grillwork guarded the compound's privacy. A bell rope dangled on one of the iron sheets. Only a distant tolling responded to his repeated tugging. After several tugs, he pushed his weight against the gates, and the rusty padlock disintegrated. The gates swung open, but there was no sound from within. Inside, an old ornamental pool filled with stagnant water, dominated the bleak courtyard. Six giant goldfish floated with their white bellies upward on the cloudy, brown surface. Beyond the grass-roofed complex, a forest-like bushed court ascended the hillside, which was overrun with overgrown vegetation in complete neglect. He walked into the larger hut of the complex.

As Father Claudio's eyes became adjusted to the darkness of the indoor light, he noted a young man sprawled across the table with his sightless eyes glaring in his blue-tinged face. A puddle of bilious yellow-green matter on the tile floor swarmed with iridescent blow-flies. The air was heavy with a sickly sweet stench, compounded of vomit, feces, urine, food and the feral reek of rats. It was all he could do to do to keep from retching. He walked through the maze of rooms and courtyards in awed silence. The only sound was of a barking dog.

The dog's golden brown hair swept the filthy, splattered floor, while his bright eyes and nervous movements showed vigorous health. Father Claudio stopped to pet him and the dog snapped at him. Claudio penetrated the innermost courtyard, where the women's quarters were protected by a round moongate. The gate stood open, and a wrinkled crone in black trousers and white tunic hobbled into the courtyard. She was almost bald, and the gray hair above an intelligent, walnut face had been pulled back into a tight fist for more than half a century.

"Father, I am so happy you have come. I am old and helpless, and the few of us here cannot take care of all of the sick people."

A slender woman in her early forties lay on a cot that had been carried outdoors. Her pale skin was taut over her high cheek bones, and her eyes glittered with fever. Then the rest began to file out into the courtyard. These unfortunates, afflicted with this dreaded disease, just stood there in silence, looking at Father Claudio with eyes full of hope, awaiting his blessing. He entered the building. The floor of the room was covered with dust, and the room smelled sour. Old rats came out boldly to dart about, searching for morsels of food, their eyes bright and black as beads. It had been raining for weeks, and the walls of stone were moist and dripping with a green mossy slime sunk into them. Cots were closely set next to each other as in barracks. A tallow candle burned with a low sullen flame, as though oppressed by the stinking air.

On one of the cots far from the door, sprawled a morose woman who stared dully at others. One side of her mouth screwed up in a faint smile and there were larger open sores on her face and breasts. Now and again, she coughed with a hollow, racking sound as if she would bring up her very guts.

Another woman sat wrapped in her cotton garment, with one hand tightly grasping the barking dog who had taken refuge upon her lap. No one spoke a word, but fidgeted nervously as Father Claudio gazed upon them. From everywhere about them came muffled sounds of shouts and groans and cries of pain, and Father Claudio knew there were many more unfortunates he must meet. He noticed other suffering humans strewn around the room, each of them wrapped in their own pain. They seemed unconscious of their whereabouts and hope was gone from their faces. A woman, perhaps fifty years old, came into the room. Her almost-white hair was lifeless as straw and skewed into a hard knot high on the crown of her head. She wore a soiled blouse and a dark blue cotton skirt with a long red apron tied over it. Slung about her hips were several towels and a pair of scissors. She carried a candle stuck in a bottle, and before turning around to look at them, she set it on the shelf.

A huge gray cat followed her, pushing against her legs and arching his back, giving out a low satisfied rumble. Then, all at once, she caught sight of Father Claudio, the priest assigned to take over the place and her job as well. It was about time. She was tired of trying to make this infested pesthole livable without help or funds. Let the church try it for a while and see what they could do! It was time for her to return to her Brittany, to spend the last years of her life in peace. The cat now sat patiently at her feet, wide eyed and flicking just the tip of his tail.

"I am Father Claudio," he said, as he extended his hand in greeting. She ignored the gesture. "Thank God you've arrived, and none too soon. I am fully packed. I had planned to leave tomorrow on the boat, whether you had arrived or not. This jewel is now yours. Let's see what you can do!" With head on high, she waved her hand at him, but did not glance around and simply walked away.

This was the only time he had met or would see the mistress of The Lady of Solace. Father Claudio heard a great disturbance emanating from the darkest part of the room. He heard someone shouting "Father, Father, come; there is an emergency and someone needs your help."

He rushed to the back of the room, his candle in hand and, to his surprise, on filthy and soiled linens, a woman was giving birth to a new life. The baby's head began to appear like a red wrinkled apple and, a few moments later, a boy was born—a moving, breathing proof of existence that reminded Father Claudio that this must be the signal from God. "A new life, a new beginning," Father Claudio whispered. "Tomorrow we begin."

He now found himself suddenly adrift, lost and filled with a cold apprehension of the future. The lives and well-being of these people lay in his hands and, hopefully, with God's help and a great deal of work, he could help these people.

It had stopped raining the day before. The night had been cold so that there was a crust on the mud. A pale, but hot sun sifted down through the gray blue sky and there were whiffs of clouds overhead, too white and thin to threaten more immediate rain. This would be a great day to get started.

Oh, how they labored, how they worked to get the place in order. The work was hard and the hours were long, but it was most urgent to get it done as soon as possible. After one week of hard labor in the tropical heat, Father Claudio's body began to understand true exhaustion. His face was wet with sweat, so that drops slid along his jaw as he moved like a man half drunk. His muscles were so tired they seemed almost useless. There was a pounding head-ache over his eyes, and a dull aching pain had filled his back and loins and went down into his legs. The work had to be done, and he could not stop until it was finished.

If he had not been such a dedicated person, he would have given up the first day. Pestilence raged all over the colony with only a very few to help him. During the first week, eighteen corpses were counted. The death cart had refused to pick up these lost souls, and it was up to Father Claudio with some of his over-worked people to dig the graves and bury them.

He had entered this place to atone for his great sin against God. Every day he met death head-on and prayed that one day soon he, too, would be among those being buried. Now began the long and tragic travail of despair, lightened only by the fortitude of his flock, these poor afflicted humans.

It became apparent that, in spite of the order of cleanliness that Father Claudio had helped to create, many innocents were still going to die. This was the will of God.

Another sad situation was the constant reminder of the underfed children and the despair of the old and the sick. He wrote to Rome and to his cardinal, desperately pleading for food, clothing and medical supplies; but only a few morsels arrived. He prayed to God constantly for His help and guidance but, unfortunately, very little help arrived. These people seemed to have been forgotten by everyone. He was helpless to combat the cumulative and gigantic job that had fallen on him.

His thoughts were interrupted by another patient's screams. The doctor had gone to town for more medicines, and Father Claudio ran toward the building that was now being used as a hospital. The patient was lying flat on his back; the quilt had fallen off, exposing his deformed body and he was moving restlessly. His eyes closed tightly, and his face contorted as the nun bent over him with the quilt again. He looked up at her and then, suddenly, he reached out and grabbed her wrist, giving it a savage jerk. "What are you doing?" His voice was thickened and hoarse and the words slurred one over the other. The green gray iris of is eyes glittered, but the eyeballs were congested and red.

"Help me. I am dying," he almost shouted the words and pulled her arm toward him furiously. The sister was scared, for she thought he was losing his mind. She looked towards Father Claudio with desperate, pleading eyes. Father Claudio bent down towards the tortured man, gently opened his fist, and released the sister's arm, and answered him in a calm, reasonable voice, "Please lie still and rest. God and I are with you." The sister began to pray. The patient took a deep long breath, and quietly expired. No matter how often he met death face to face, Father Claudio could never seem to get accustomed to it.

Then, one fortunate day, the Capuchin Monks arrived—those wonderful dedicated men were not fearful of catching the disease, but interested in helping those less fortunate than themselves. They were truly a Godsend. They taught the healthier patients how to work the land and, at harvest time, the food was most happily appreciated. They got a few cows and chickens and even a pig. Life certainly had turned around for all of them. God was kind, God was good, and hope returned into their hearts. In retrospect, he had been fortunate in the fact that two nuns had been sent to him. They were dedicated women, and he found them indispensable.

Finally, after many years of starvation, work and suffering, "The Lady of Solace Refuge" seemed to be flourishing. At least they all had enough to eat and even a doctor on call.

Though this refuge was treated to major repairs, its under-equipped barracks still remained damp and drafty on cold days. He dreamed of a real hospital, where these incurables could obtain medical and spiritual comfort in their last agonies. It would cost a great deal of money, and to find such a sum became his long-range goal.

Father Claudio was summoned by Rome. They had not forgotten him, after all, and he had been closely monitored all of these years. He was instructed to visit another Leper Colony—this one in far-away Algeria—and see what changes and suggestions for improvement he could make.

Father Claudio had become quite fond of his flock at The Lady of Solace Refuge, and had begun to almost feel happy again. After all, they were his family now. God must have known of his resigned, almost contented situation, for now he was faced with a two-month voyage to parts unknown. Who knew what he would find?

CHAPTER THIRTY-FIVE

Misericordia

It was almost dusk when he alighted from the ship and set foot in Algiers. He started walking up the dirt road. After a seven-mile climb, he reached the gate and read a small sign bearing the single word, "Misericordia." Oh! How this reminded him of his first arrival at Lady of Solace, thirty years ago! He entered a desolate courtyard, and saw a rambling building, dreary with dust, and mud clogging the steps. In the falling rain and the low wind mourning through the trees, he noted a single dimly lit window on the second floor of the house, which created an almost sinister atmosphere. He opened the front door and walked in. Stale deodorants lay heavy in the warm air. A candle stuck in a baking soda tin threw flickering shadows on a number of closed doors.

Listening at the first floor, he heard a sepulchral groan. From the second floor came a gasping, low cry, and then, frightened whimpers. A nun glided out of the shadows, carrying a sick room utensil.

"May I see the sister in charge here?" asked the weary Father. His priestly garb was passport enough.

"You will find Sister Maria Annunziata on the second floor, last door at the left."

The smell of deodorant became heavier as Father Claudio mounted the creaking stairway. He found himself tiptoeing down a corridor dimly lit by a simple taper, burning before a plaster figure of The Virgin Mary. At the last door, he listened to a strange antiphon, one voice soothed while the other answered with weak retching.

Father Claudio rapped gently and then opened the door. A blasting stench of putrescence struck his nostrils. The odor of death came from a ghastly yellow-fleshed human being—whether man or woman, it was impossible to tell—propped up on pillows. The eyes were staring in pain. The lower jaw sagged uncontrollably as greenish bile poured across from its broken dam.

Kneeling by the bedside, a gray-habited nun gazed with infinite tenderness and a suffering heart at the horrible, pain-driven face on the pillow. That face must have once been very beautiful. In her hands, the nun held an aged basin to catch the fetid trickle oozing from the death's head. The nun was not praying or exhorting. From her lips came a loving murmur, the sounds only a mother might whisper to a feverish child. Only one voice could speak like that! Roxanne…

Roxanne…Roxanne!!!!!!!!!

The nun lifted her wet, shiny eyes to Father Claudio, recognized him, and made a little signal, part headshake, part finger, to her lips and said, "In a moment it will be over. Please, Father, will you give him absolution?"

Without hesitation, Father Claudio opened up the small case he was carrying and took out the Holy Oils of extreme unction. Setting them on a small table nearby, he dipped his thumb in the sacramental oil and carried it to the dying person's eyelids. He anointed those eyelids in the form of a cross, saying in Latin as he did so, "Through this holy unction, and his most tender mercy, may the Lord pardon thee whatsoever sins thou hast committed by sight." "What sins could there be?" thought Sister Maria Annunziata.

Gently, he anointed the eroded ears, nostrils, the swollen lips and the deformed hands of this most unfortunate being. Then he motioned to the nun, "Lift the quilt so I can anoint his feet," the gesture said. Eyes blurred with tears, she exposed the stubs where legs should have been. Father Claudio stepped back, completely shocked at the sight. With hands trembling, he completed with a touch of sacred oil to the remaining scar tissue, making the sign of the cross where once was an instep.

"Through this holy unction, and his most tender mercy, may the Lord pardon thee whatsoever sins thou hast committed by thy footsteps. Amen."

The two people of the cloth looked at each other, both suffering deeply and silently praying for this soul as the dying being, like a thin veil from its face, eyes, ears, lips, and hands were freed from their sensual burdens. Feet that were not there, that had never walked in any way but righteousness became clay. His soul rose from the mental ash of the body and leaped in flame, to join the fellowship of saints, martyrs and God.

With oils and bag in hand, Father Claudio left. He was glad to close the door. This poor soul had suffered so much and he was overwhelmed with great pain for the deceased. In the stifling corridor, he knelt before The Virgin's Statue and prayed for the soul that Maria Annunziata was leading toward release.

The end must have come peacefully. Candle in hand, Roxanne came out of the sick room and beckoned Claudio to follow her down the dim hallway. At the top of the stairway she faced him. In the taper light he could see that her face had lost the contours of her youth and the radiance of its beauty. Her hands were roughened by menial labor. At fifty-one, the beautiful Countess was prematurely old. What kind of Hell had she suffered to make her look this way? Yet, her very sad eyes were illuminated from within.

"Oh! How I prayed to see you just one more time before I died!" she said. Scold me for such prayers, but I couldn't help it. There was something I had to tell you."

"Scold you? I have no wish to scold you. You are the one I must ask forgiveness of—you and my God. Tell me, whatever happened to you and what made you decide to become a nun and give yourself to God? What type of colony is this and why was I called to visit it?" There were so many questions he wanted to ask.

"This is Misericordia, a house of last breathings, a refuge for those destitute, incurables who would otherwise die uncared for—a colony so poor, and without aid from anyone and not enough volunteers to help.

"But each colony should look after his own"

"Misericordia is religion and humanity. Patients who are dying of the last stages of the disease, where all medicines are powerless to ease their pain and nothing can be done for their bodies, we try at the end to give them what comfort we can."

"How long have you been here?"

"Almost twenty years."

"But why here? Why in a Leper Colony?"

"Because our son fell victim of this dreaded disease."

Father Claudio could neither move nor speak as no words could discharge his feelings of astonishment and unworthiness. Involuntary mechanisms, far below the level of consciousness, took possession of him. A fine sweat broke from the roots of his hair. The blood momentarily withdrew from his face and then climbed again in a hot tide. He fell to his knees, in front of the woman—the woman who he had always loved.

White and visibly shaken, he looked up at her, eyes begging forgiveness. He continued gazing at Sister Maria Annunziata and completely broke down with tears that shook his whole body.

"Yes, Father Claudio, we were not the only ones who had to pay for our sin. Our beautiful son, the sweetest being that ever lived, he too suffered a life of pain.

"He was so handsome and looked so much like you. That infuriated the Count each time he saw him. The Count began to abuse our little 'Angel.' That's what I called him, for he was a true angel. We ran away, but the years in Paris streets were not kind to Angel's health and, at the age of ten, he was diagnosed with leprosy. That is when we came here, for both of us to die."

"Then, tell me. Where is my son, my poor, unfortunate son? Tell me, Roxanne, where is he?

The question brought her back to reality. She was panting like a wounded animal, exhausted, moving from side to side in a delirium of pain. The grinding of her teeth told him more than his agonizing tears. With lips cracked with dry saliva, she spoke in a dull soft voice.

"Oh, dearest Claudio, you just gave your son the last rites a few minutes ago."

He wanted to throw himself on the floor. His lips were shaping desperate words. God had certainly punished them for their sin. But their child was innocent. Why him? Why did he have to pay for the sin of his parents? Father Claudio wanted to die, why did God not take his life, too? And in mortal anguish, he collapsed. That fatal day, everything inside Sister Maria Annunziata and Father Claudio died completely. Every day from then on would be torture and pain.

He left the next day to return to his colony. Travel in Africa was difficult and uncomfortable, and he was a broken human being. He was desperately in need of God but God refused to help him. He was anxious to get back to The Lady of Solace and his own private Hell.

CHAPTER THIRTY-SIX

Another Battle

The time came at last when his office, his little church and the small hospital and colony no longer required the utmost expenditure of his physical and nervous energy. It was at this time that Father Claudio, himself, was stricken by the crippling disease. A sharp bout of pneumonia, induced by the strain of chronic fatigue, sent him to bed in early October. The medical care from Doctor Mandreut, plus the prayers of his congregation, were apparently speeding the patient to an uneventful recovery.

After a month he was able to walk about the room. Already, he had begun to plague Doctor Mandreut with his restless convalescence.

He questioned, "When can I get back to work?"

"You'll be able to celebrate Mass on All Saints Day."

Father Claudio noticed a curious swelling of his right leg, a distention so marked that he could not tie his shoes. "I'll say nothing about it. Try to walk it off," he said to himself. He managed to struggle through Mass without revealing the condition of his leg to anyone. After lunch, he was glad to get back into bed. The next day his leg was swollen to the knee. Alarmed, he called Doctor Mandreut.

The old physician made a thorough examination of the swollen limb. He pressed the calf, put his fingers under the arch of Claudio's knee and asked humorously, "Been in any jungles lately?"

In spite of the light conversation, the doctor was worried it might be Wicheria Bancrofti, the parasites that cause elephantiasis, or Leprosy, which was so prevalent all around them. Doctor Mandreut was off on another diagnostic tack. This time, he applied a stethoscope to Claudio's heart, listened long and brought his grizzled head up reassuringly. "It's certainly not cardiac, Father."

"That's fine, it's not my heart. Then, what is it?"

"I'll be asking the questions today. Anyone in your family ever have trouble with their legs?"

"My father had varicose veins." Doctor Mandreut went into a room to ponder and came out on the tentative side. "I believe you might have phlebitis."

"Is that good or bad?"

"It can be dangerous."

"Can it cause death?"

"Now, don't start painting the devil on the wall.

We'll keep you off your feet for a couple of weeks and see what happens."

"A couple of weeks? That's impossible!" I have all these people to take care of, a baptism, confessions, Mass and prayers." Father Claudio flung his hands impatiently.

"It can wait. Bed rest is nature's best remedy." And bed rest it was for two trying weeks. Doctor Mandreut bandaged the swollen leg, kept it elevated and put his patient on a bland diet. Contemptuous of slow treatment, the swelling increased. Claudio's leg was now enormous; it throbbed painfully and would not sustain his weight when he attempted to walk. Doctor Mandreut took tests of Claudio's urine and a specimen of fluid drained from his swollen leg and sent this to the nearest laboratory, about fifty miles away. Finally, the results came back. Doctor Mandreut sat down beside Father Claudio's bed, "My diagnosis agrees with the lab tests. You've got phlebitis. That is an inflammation of the veins deep in your leg. The picture is complicated by the Leprosy in your system, which is causing this lymphatic involvement."

He need not explain anymore. Claudio was very well acquainted with this disease and what it could do to the human body. "Will my leg continue to look and feel like a sausage; is this the end of the story?"

"The acute phase might pass spontaneously; cures

have been reported." Doctor Mandreut was encouraging. "We'll try everything—arsenics, drainage, heat, and more bed rest."

Father Claudio was disconsolate. "That's about all we can do. You must have patience, Father Claudio."

Patience! Medicine is easiest to prescribe, hardest to take. Patience is the calm enduring of catastrophe or pain. Patience is one of the moral virtues, a special gift of the Holy Ghost. "I'll try," promised Father Claudio.

Like most men who enjoyed the blessing of good health all of their life, Father Claudio was a poor patient. Flat on his back, legs propped up on pillows, in this hot humid tropical weather, he passed through irritability to bitterness, and through bitterness to desperation. For the first month he felt like a tortured victim, strapped to the floor of a belfry while monstrous chimes tolled "doom, doom," above his head.

Meanwhile, his ecclesiastical duties accumulated and lapsed. Some he handled from his bed, such as one-at-a-time confessions and, later, his bed was wheeled outdoors so he would be able to say Mass. Some he delegated to the kind monks and to his assistant, all of whom responded with selfless devotion. By means of these auxiliary helpers, Claudio managed from his bed to keep the colony going.

Most of his parishioners visited him. These were beacons that helped Claudio's passage across the seas of illness. Their friendship was immeasurably sweet, a temporary prop to his loneliness, a corporal proof of love.

Gradually, however, Father Claudio began to realize that mortal friends, with all of their sustaining strength, would not float him over the sunken ledges of despondency. Only one friend could do that, and where was that friend now?

Once in a midnight hour of querulous misery, Father Claudio cried out, "Lord, Lord why has thou forsaken me?" To his anguished cry, no answer came. God's silence was stony; his face was turned away.

For five hot bedridden months, Father Claudio's leg remained a swollen useless thing, suspended in a leather harness and a fever hung on, too. Three times a day the waxen fingers of Sister Regina Dorata placed a thermometer between Father Claudio's lips. Then, after a tranquil greeting of the mercury, she would make a note of it on his chart. How maddeningly composed the woman was.

His mind wandered back to the day he first arrived here, and remembered the terrible conditions in which those sick ones had been forced to live, without comfort of even a clean sheet to lie on! What a pesthole it had been, but with the help of God, today it was livable. He was proud of the fact that he had a hand in this accomplishment. But had he lost the gift of humility feeling this way? Had he forgotten that suffering was God's physic to swollen pride? Crimson shame tinged his cheeks. After much soul searching, he realized he had to make that desperate struggle for acceptance of The Father's Will.

In daily communion, by incessant prayer and from pages of saintly works, Father Claudio sought to place his life in God's keeping. He almost succeeded. For an hour or two, he would recapture the power of accepting tribulation. A blessed response would permeate his heart and mind. He had learned that a man may give away all his goods, yet that is nothing, and do many deeds of penitence, yet that is a small thing.

But he had to utterly give himself up, and retain nothing of self-love. It was a man who retained little of self-love on whom Doctor Mandreut performed the surgical operation. His leg had to be cut off to prevent the spreading of the infection.

During these trying and difficult times, somehow, Roxanne's image never faded; her voice did not grow dimmer and, like a slow-drawing wave, refused to retreat down the beaches of Father Claudio's heart and leave him standing before the tabernacle alone. She was within him until the end.

Father Claudio died the death of a Leper two years later, just like his son and the patients he had tried to help.

Sister Maria Annunziata continued her work of mercy, trying to console all those who needed her. Yet, no one was ever able to console her suffering soul.

THE END

Re-enactment of the story of the Padrone from Book Two
(1989 Carnival)

Epilogue

Today The Castel sits above the hill, as she has for the last five centuries, like an old lady guarding the town's inhabitants.

The new, well-educated generation is unaware of the folklore, the atrocities that occurred there. No longer do they know or believe in ghosts. To them, this historical building only represents their town. Little do they know the ceremony they re-enact at carnival time is the second tale in this book.

Unfortunately, folklore is no longer stylish. They are losing a piece of the town's history. And when you lose your folklore, you lose part of yourself and part of life.

I have been returning, every few years. Each time I see my old home, I cry . . . but I refuse to enter it, for I must remember the way it was!

The Story Behind This Novel

The author of *The Sins of Castel du Mont*, Rosemary Bracco Greenbaum Kohler had often been told she was the first legitimate child born in the castle. This edifice had originally been built toward the end of the sixteenth century by the reigning pope. The U-shaped, fortress-style castle was intended to serve travelers departing from Rome to Paris. This was the last resting place before entering the Great St. Bernard Pass that extended from Courmayeur (now Italy) under the Alps to Chamonix, France.

The castle had been owned by the Vatican until the end of the eighteenth century, when it was passed on to a padrone who had performed numerous favors for and contributed a great deal of money to the church.

Rosemary loved living there, in spite of all the stories she often heard about the castle being haunted.

"Haunted? Have you ever seen a ghost?" people often asked.

"Doesn't everyone have their own ghost?" she

would reply. She had heard and remembered the numerous tales of the atrocities that people gossiped about, which had occurred ages before.

In 1934, the family moved to her mother's country, the United States of America, and settled in New York City. She had nearly forgotten her haunted castle until 1964, when she returned for a visit to introduce her husband and three young sons to the place she had been born. The old memories returned and began to haunt her once more. She started writing what she remembered, but found her memory was incomplete. She had to speak to the old people in her town, the ones who still might remember some of the folklore that had been passed down for generations—tales now forgotten by the new generation. She needed to travel to talk to those few who still might remember.

She took courses in the travel business, a new field that was in its infancy and was struggling to survive. After spending six months working in a travel agency, she opened her own agency. Luck was on her side, for in the early days of the industry, the airlines, hotels, and car rental agencies were all too eager to offer flights, accommodations and rentals free of charge in order to familiarize travel agents with their products. She took advantage of their invitations and with the aid of friends was able to obtain a list of older seniors between the ages of eighty to one hundred years old, people who remembered the timeworn tales and were kind enough to share them with her.

Every two weeks, she flew on Friday afternoon to Milano, Italy, rented a car and drove the two hours west to her hometown. On Saturday, recorder in hand, she interviewed as many aged people as possible. Sunday morning, she boarded the plane for the return flight to New York. Monday morning found her back at work.

With the help of her close friends, Antonio Antoniotti and his wife, Maria, she was able to gather much information. She swore them to secrecy until the book had been published. Unfortunately, they never got to see the completed book.

The older generation only spoke Piedmontese, a dialect of her home region. She had no trouble deciphering it and translating it to English. Working diligently, as with a puzzle, she found that the saga was divided into three different stories. The middle tale is the one that was being reenacted every year at Carnival time.

By 1994, she had finished the book. Her husband died and the book was shelved. It was not until 2014 that she finally decided it should be published. With no intention of hurting anyone's pride or feelings, she simply wrote the stories verbatim, exactly as they had been told to her. She always felt that the folklore saga of the castle had to be told because if one loses its folklore, he also loses part of himself.

About the Author

osemary Bracco Greenbaum Kohler was born in a castle in northern Italy, near the French border. The historic edifice was owned by her grandfather. She attended preschool at "The Asilo" at the age of two. At age three, she learned to paint in watercolors, personally guided by the Mother Superior. She attended public school in Italy, where she wrote and illustrated her first book when she was nine years old. The teacher, Mrs. Rita Di Benedetto, entered the book in a contest that reached across all of Italy and won one of the first ten prizes.

Kohler continued her education after her arrival in the United States, including private art lessons with the Bohemian artists during the Great Depression (1934). She became a graduate of a four-year course in dress designing at Washington Irving Art School in New York City.

She worked for Fleisher and Disney Studios as a pen and ink artist on such films at *Betty Boop, Little Lulu, Popeye,* and *Snow White and the Seven Dwarfs.* She was president and art teacher at her private art studio for thirty-five years. She traveled around the globe learning and expanding her knowledge of art and the understanding of people and customs. For four years, she counseled senior citizens at Manhattanville College in Rye, New York, on techniques of "How to Write Your Memoirs." In the end, all had enough material ready for their book printing.

After eighteen years of hard work, she had her first book published, *A Life of Mosaics: A Photo Album/Autobiography,* which goes back four generations from paternal great grandmother, who was an Italian Saphardic Jew, to her maternal great greandmother, who was an American Indian (Iroquios). The book is the family tree for her three grandchildren. Her second book, *The Sins of Castel du Mont,* is the folklore of the castle that was her birthplace.

At age seventy-nine, she developed macular degeneration in both eyes and lost fifty percent of her eyesight in one week. Presently she receives, from her ophthalmologist, a monthly injection in each eye to retain what eyesight she has left. She is also hearing impaired.

Yet at the age of ninety, she is always ready to take on new challenges in both art and writing, and keeps busy lecturing on her books and her art, including another book she has written, *There is Life After Macular Degeneration.* In her own words, "I find that I am busier than ever and enjoy every minute I am alive."